Alice Munro

VINTAGE **MUNRO**

Alice Munro grew up in Wingham, Ontario, and attended the University of Western Ontario. She has published fourteen collections of stories as well as a novel, *Lives of Girls and Women*. During her distinguished career she has been the recipient of many awards and prizes, including three of Canada's Governor General's Literary Awards and two Giller Prizes, the Rea Award for the Short Story, the Lannan Literary Award, the W. H. Smith Literary Award, the National Book Critics Circle Award, and the Man Booker International Prize. Her stories have appeared in *The New Yorker*, *The Atlantic*, *The Paris Review*, and other publications, and her collections have been translated into thirteen languages. She was awarded the Nobel Prize in Literature in 2013.

BOOKS BY ALICE MUNRO

Dear Life
Too Much Happiness
The View from Castle Rock
Away from Her
Carried Away
Runaway
Vintage Munro
Hateship, Friendship, Courtship, Loveship, Marriage
The Love of a Good Woman
Selected Stories
Open Secrets
Friend of My Youth
The Progress of Love
The Moons of Jupiter
The Beggar Maid
Something I've Been Meaning to Tell You
Lives of Girls and Women
Dance of the Happy Shades

VINTAGE MUNRO

Alice Munro

VINTAGE BOOKS

A Division of Random House LLC

New York

VINTAGE BOOKS EDITIONS, 2004, 2014

Library of Congress Cataloging-in-Publication Data
Munro, Alice.
[Short stories. Selections]
Vintage Munro / Alice Munro.—1st Vintage Books ed.
p. cm.
Contents: Moons of Jupiter—The progress of love—Differently—Carried away—Hateship, friendship, courtship, loveship, marriage—In Sight of the Lake.
1. Canada—Social life and customs—Fiction. I. Title.
PR9199.3.M8A6 2004
813'.54—dc21
2003053825

Vintage ISBN 978-0-8041-7356-8

Book design by JoAnne Metsch

www.vintagebooks.com

Printed in the United States of America
10 9 8 7 6 5 4 3 2 1

CONTENTS

THE MOONS OF JUPITER
from *The Moons of Jupiter*   *3*

THE PROGRESS OF LOVE
from *The Progress of Love*   *24*

DIFFERENTLY
from *Friend of My Youth*   *58*

CARRIED AWAY
from *Open Secrets*   *88*

HATESHIP, FRIENDSHIP, COURTSHIP, LOVESHIP,
MARRIAGE from *Hateship, Friendship,
Courtship, Loveship, Marriage*   *137*

IN SIGHT OF THE LAKE
from *Dear Life*   *192*

THE NOBEL PRIZE IN LITERATURE
2013: PRESENTATION SPEECH   *207*

VINTAGE MUNRO

THE MOONS OF JUPITER

I found my father in the heart wing, on the eighth floor of Toronto General Hospital. He was in a semi-private room. The other bed was empty. He said that his hospital insurance covered only a bed in the ward, and he was worried that he might be charged extra.

"I never asked for a semi-private," he said.

I said the wards were probably full.

"No. I saw some empty beds when they were wheeling me by."

"Then it was because you had to be hooked up to that thing," I said. "Don't worry. If they're going to charge you extra, they tell you about it."

"That's likely it," he said. "They wouldn't want those doo-hickeys set up in the wards. I guess I'm covered for that kind of thing."

I said I was sure he was.

He had wires taped to his chest. A small screen hung over his head. On the screen a bright jagged line was continually being written. The writing was accompanied by a nervous electronic beeping. The behavior of his heart was on display. I tried to ignore it. It seemed to me that paying such close attention—in fact, dramatizing what ought to be a most secret activity—was asking for trouble. Anything exposed that way was apt to flare up and go crazy. My father did not seem to mind. He said they had him on tranquillizers. You know, he said, the happy pills. He did seem calm and optimistic.

It had been a different story the night before. When I brought him into the hospital, to the emergency room, he had been pale and closemouthed. He had opened the car door and stood up and said quietly, "Maybe you better get me one of those wheelchairs." He used the voice he always used in a crisis. Once, our chimney caught on fire; it was on a Sunday afternoon and I was in the dining room pinning together a dress I was making. He came in and said in that same matter-of-fact, warning voice, "Janet. Do you know where there's some baking powder?" He wanted it to throw on the fire. Afterwards he said, "I guess it was your fault—sewing on Sunday."

I had to wait for over an hour in the emergency waiting room. They summoned a heart specialist who was in the hospital, a young man. He called me out into the hall and explained to me that one of the valves of my father's heart had deteriorated so badly that there ought to be an immediate operation.

I asked him what would happen otherwise.

"He'd have to stay in bed," the doctor said.

"How long?"

"Maybe three months."

"I meant, how long would he live?"

"That's what I meant, too," the doctor said.

I went to see my father. He was sitting up in bed in a curtained-off corner. "It's bad, isn't it?" he said. "Did he tell you above the valve?"

"It's not as bad as it could be," I said. Then I repeated, even exaggerated, anything hopeful the doctor had said. "You're not in any immediate danger. Your physical condition is good, otherwise."

"Otherwise," said my father, gloomily.

I was tired from the drive—all the way up to Dalgleish, to get him, and back to Toronto since noon—and worried about getting the rented car back on time, and irritated by an article I had been reading in a magazine in the waiting room. It was about another writer, a woman younger, better-looking, probably more talented than I am. I had been in England for two months and so I had not seen this article before, but it crossed my mind while I was reading that my father would have. I could hear him saying, Well, I didn't see anything about you in *Maclean's*. And if he had read something about me he would say, Well, I didn't think too much of that write-up. His tone would be humorous and indulgent but would produce in me a familiar dreariness of spirit. The message I got from him was simple: Fame must be striven for, then apologized for. Getting or not getting it, you will be to blame.

I was not surprised by the doctor's news. I was prepared to hear something of the sort and was pleased with myself for taking it calmly, just as I would be pleased with myself for dressing a wound or looking down from the frail balcony of a high building. I thought, Yes, it's time; there has to be something, here it is. I did not feel any of the protest I would have felt twenty, even ten, years before. When I saw from my father's face that he felt it—that refusal leapt up in him as readily as if he had been thirty or forty years younger—my heart hardened, and I spoke with a kind of badgering cheerfulness. "Otherwise is plenty," I said.

———

The next day he was himself again.

That was how I would have put it. He said it appeared to him now that the young fellow, the doctor, might have been a bit too eager to operate. "A bit knife-happy," he said. He was both mocking and showing off the hospital slang. He said that another doctor had examined him, an older man, and had given it as his opinion that rest and medication might do the trick.

I didn't ask what trick.

"He says I've got a defective valve, all right. There's certainly some damage. They wanted to know if I had rheumatic fever when I was a kid. I said I didn't think so. But half the time then you weren't diagnosed what you had. My father was not one for getting the doctor."

The thought of my father's childhood, which I always pictured as bleak and dangerous—the poor farm, the scared sisters, the harsh father—made me less resigned to his dying. I thought of him running away to work on the lake boats, running along the railway tracks, toward Goderich, in the evening light. He used to tell about that trip. Somewhere along the track he found a quince tree. Quince trees are rare in our part of the country; in fact, I have never seen one. Not even the one my father found, though he once took us on an expedition to look for it. He thought he knew the crossroad it was near, but we could not find it. He had not been able to eat the fruit, of course, but he had been impressed by its existence. It made him think he had got into a new part of the world.

The escaped child, the survivor, an old man trapped here by his leaky heart. I didn't pursue these thoughts. I didn't care to think of his younger selves. Even his bare torso, thick and white—he had the body of a workingman of his generation, seldom exposed to the sun—was a danger to me; it looked so strong and young. The wrinkled neck, the age-freckled hands and arms, the narrow, courteous head, with its thin gray hair and mustache, were more what I was used to.

"Now, why would I want to get myself operated on?" said my father reasonably. "Think of the risk at my age, and what for? A few years at the outside. I think the best thing for me to do is go home and take it easy. Give in gracefully. That's all you can do, at my age. Your attitude changes, you know. You go through some mental changes. It seems more natural."

"What does?" I said.

"Well, death does. You can't get more natural than that. No, what I mean, specifically, is not having the operation."

"That seems more natural?"

"Yes."

"It's up to you," I said, but I did approve. This was what I would have expected of him. Whenever I told people about my father I stressed his independence, his self-sufficiency, his forbearance. He worked in a factory, he worked in his garden, he read history books. He could tell you about the Roman emperors or the Balkan wars. He never made a fuss.

Judith, my younger daughter, had come to meet me at Toronto Airport two days before. She had brought the boy she was living with, whose name was Don. They were driving to Mexico in the morning, and while I was in Toronto I was to stay in their apartment. For the time being, I live in Vancouver. I sometimes say I have my headquarters in Vancouver.

"Where's Nichola?" I said, thinking at once of an accident or an overdose. Nichola is my older daughter. She used to be a student at the Conservatory, then she became a cocktail waitress, then she was out of work. If she had been at the airport, I would probably have said something wrong. I would have asked her what her plans were, and she would have gracefully

brushed back her hair and said, "Plans?"—as if that was a word
I had invented.

"I knew the first thing you'd say would be about Nichola,"
Judith said.

"It wasn't. I said hello and I—"

"We'll get your bag," Don said neutrally.

"Is she all right?"

"I'm sure she is," said Judith, with a fabricated air of amusement. "You wouldn't look like that if I was the one who wasn't
here."

"Of course I would."

"You wouldn't. Nichola is the baby of the family. You
know, she's four years older than I am."

"I ought to know."

Judith said she did not know where Nichola was exactly. She
said Nichola had moved out of her apartment (that dump!) and
had actually telephoned (which is quite a deal, you might say,
Nichola phoning) to say she wanted to be incommunicado for
a while but she was fine.

"I told her you would worry," said Judith more kindly on
the way to their van. Don walked ahead carrying my suitcase.
"But don't. She's all right, believe me."

Don's presence made me uncomfortable. I did not like him
to hear these things. I thought of the conversations they must
have had, Don and Judith. Or Don and Judith and Nichola, for
Nichola and Judith were sometimes on good terms. Or Don
and Judith and Nichola and others whose names I did not even
know. They would have talked about me. Judith and Nichola
comparing notes, relating anecdotes; analyzing, regretting, blam-
ing, forgiving. I wished I'd had a boy and a girl. Or two boys.
They wouldn't have done that. Boys couldn't possibly know so
much about you.

I did the same thing at that age. When I was the age Judith is now I talked with my friends in the college cafeteria or, late at night, over coffee in our cheap rooms. When I was the age Nichola is now I had Nichola herself in a carry-cot or squirming in my lap, and I was drinking coffee again all the rainy Vancouver afternoons with my one neighborhood friend, Ruth Boudreau, who read a lot and was bewildered by her situation, as I was. We talked about our parents, our childhoods, though for some time we kept clear of our marriages. How thoroughly we dealt with our fathers and mothers, deplored their marriages, their mistaken ambitions or fear of ambition, how competently we filed them away, defined them beyond any possibility of change. What presumption.

I looked at Don walking ahead. A tall ascetic-looking boy, with a St. Francis cap of black hair, a precise fringe of beard. What right did he have to hear about me, to know things I myself had probably forgotten? I decided that his beard and hairstyle were affected.

Once, when my children were little, my father said to me, "You know those years you were growing up—well, that's all just a kind of a blur to me. I can't sort out one year from another." I was offended. I remembered each separate year with pain and clarity. I could have told how old I was when I went to look at the evening dresses in the window of Benbow's Ladies' Wear. Every week through the winter a new dress, spotlit—the sequins and tulle, the rose and lilac, sapphire, daffodil—and me a cold worshipper on the slushy sidewalk. I could have told how old I was when I forged my mother's signature on a bad report card, when I had measles, when we papered the front room. But the years when Judith and Nichola were little, when I lived with their father—yes, blur is the word for it. I remember hanging out diapers, bringing in and folding diapers; I can recall the kitchen counters of two houses and where the clothesbasket sat. I remember the televi-

sion programs—*Popeye the Sailor, The Three Stooges, Funorama.*
When *Funorama* came on it was time to turn on the lights and
cook supper. But I couldn't tell the years apart. We lived outside Vancouver in a dormitory suburb: Dormir, Dormer, Dor-
mouse—something like that. I was sleepy all the time then;
pregnancy made me sleepy, and the night feedings, and the
West Coast rain falling. Dark dripping cedars, shiny dripping
laurel; wives yawning, napping, visiting, drinking coffee, and
folding diapers; husbands coming home at night from the city
across the water. Every night I kissed my homecoming husband in his wet Burberry and hoped he might wake me up; I
served up meat and potatoes and one of the four vegetables he
permitted. He ate with a violent appetite, then fell asleep on
the living-room sofa. We had become a cartoon couple, more
middle-aged in our twenties than we would be in middle age.

Those bumbling years are the years our children will remember all their lives. Corners of the yards I never visited will stay
in their heads.

"Did Nichola not want to see me?" I said to Judith.

"She doesn't want to see anybody, half the time," she said.
Judith moved ahead and touched Don's arm. I knew that
touch—an apology, an anxious reassurance. You touch a man
that way to remind him that you are grateful, that you realize
he is doing for your sake something that bores him or slightly
endangers his dignity. It made me feel older than grandchildren
would to see my daughter touch a man—a boy—this way. I felt
her sad jitters, could predict her supple attentions. My blunt
and stocky, blonde and candid child. Why should I think she
wouldn't be susceptible, that she would always be straightfor-
ward, heavy-footed, self-reliant? Just as I go around saying that
Nichola is sly and solitary, cold, seductive. Many people must
know things that would contradict what I say.

In the morning Don and Judith left for Mexico. I decided I

wanted to see somebody who wasn't related to me, and who didn't expect anything in particular from me. I called an old lover of mine, but his phone was answered by a machine: "This is Tom Shepherd speaking. I will be out of town for the month of September. Please record your message, name, and phone number."

Tom's voice sounded so pleasant and familiar that I opened my mouth to ask him the meaning of this foolishness. Then I hung up. I felt as if he had deliberately let me down, as if we had planned to meet in a public place and then he hadn't shown up. Once, he had done that, I remembered.

I got myself a glass of vermouth, though it was not yet noon, and I phoned my father.

"Well, of all things," he said. "Fifteen more minutes and you would have missed me."

"Were you going downtown?"

"Downtown Toronto."

He explained that he was going to the hospital. His doctor in Dalgleish wanted the doctors in Toronto to take a look at him, and had given him a letter to show them in the emergency room.

"Emergency room?" I said.

"It's not an emergency. He just seems to think this is the best way to handle it. He knows the name of a fellow there. If he was to make me an appointment, it might take weeks."

"Does your doctor know you're driving to Toronto?" I said.

"Well, he didn't say I couldn't."

The upshot of this was that I rented a car, drove to Dalgleish, brought my father back to Toronto, and had him in the emergency room by seven o'clock that evening.

Before Judith left I said to her, "You're sure Nichola knows I'm staying here?"

"Well, I told her," she said.

Sometimes the phone rang, but it was always a friend of Judith's.

"Well, it looks like I'm going to have it," my father said. This was on the fourth day. He had done a complete turnaround overnight. "It looks like I might as well."

I didn't know what he wanted me to say. I thought perhaps he looked to me for a protest, an attempt to dissuade him.

"When will they do it?" I said.

"Day after tomorrow."

I said I was going to the washroom. I went to the nurses' station and found a woman there who I thought was the head nurse. At any rate, she was gray-haired, kind, and serious-looking.

"My father's having an operation the day after tomorrow?" I said.

"Oh, yes."

"I just wanted to talk to somebody about it. I thought there'd been a sort of decision reached that he'd be better not to. I thought because of his age."

"Well, it's his decision and the doctor's." She smiled at me without condescension. "It's hard to make these decisions."

"How were his tests?"

"Well, I haven't seen them all."

I was sure she had. After a moment she said, "We have to be realistic. But the doctors here are very good."

When I went back into the room my father said, in a surprised voice, "*Shore*-less seas."

"What?" I said. I wondered if he had found out how much, or how little time he could hope for. I wondered if the pills had brought on an untrustworthy euphoria. Or if he had wanted to gamble. Once, when he was talking to me about his life, he said, "The trouble was I was always afraid to take chances."

I used to tell people that he never spoke regretfully about his life, but that was not true. It was just that I didn't listen to it. He said that he should have gone into the Army as a tradesman— he would have been better off. He said he should have gone on his own, as a carpenter, after the war. He should have got out of Dalgleish. Once, he said, "A wasted life, eh?" But he was making fun of himself, saying that, because it was such a dramatic thing to say. When he quoted poetry, too, he always had a scoffing note in his voice, to excuse the showing-off and the pleasure.

"Shoreless seas," he said again. "'Behind him lay the gray Azores, / Behind the Gates of Hercules; / Before him not the ghost of shores, / Before him only shoreless seas.' That's what was going through my head last night. But do you think I could remember what kind of seas? I could not. Lonely seas? Empty seas? I was on the right track but I couldn't get it. But there now when you came into the room and I wasn't thinking about it at all, the word popped into my head. That's always the way, isn't it? It's not all that surprising. I ask my mind a question. The answer's there, but I can't see all the connections my mind's making to get it. Like a computer. Nothing out of the way. You know, in my situation the thing is, if there's anything you can't explain right away, there's a great temptation to—well, to make a mystery out of it. There's a great temptation to believe in—You know."

"The soul?" I said, speaking lightly, feeling an appalling rush of love and recognition.

"Oh, I guess you could call it that. You know, when I first came into this room there was a pile of papers here by the bed. Somebody had left them here—one of those tabloid sort of things I never looked at. I started reading them. I'll read anything handy. There was a series running in them on personal experiences of people who had died, medically speaking— heart arrest, mostly—and had been brought back to life. It was what they remembered of the time when they were dead. Their experiences."

"Pleasant or un-?" I said.

"Oh, pleasant. Oh yes. They'd float up to the ceiling and look down on themselves and see the doctors working on them, on their bodies. Then float on further and recognize some people they knew who had died before them. Not see them exactly but sort of sense them. Sometimes there would be a humming and sometimes a sort of—what's that light that there is or color around a person?"

"Aura?"

"Yes. But without the person. That's about all they'd get time for; then they found themselves back in the body and feeling all the mortal pain and so on—brought back to life."

"Did it seem—convincing?"

"Oh, I don't know. It's all in whether you want to believe that kind of thing or not. And if you are going to believe it, take it seriously, I figure you've got to take everything else seriously that they print in those papers."

"What else do they?"

"Rubbish—cancer cures, baldness cures, bellyaching about the younger generation and the welfare bums. Tripe about movie stars."

"Oh, yes. I know."

"In my situation you have to keep a watch," he said, "or you'll start playing tricks on yourself." Then he said, "There's a few practical details we ought to get straight on," and he told me about his will, the house, the cemetery plot. Everything was simple.

"Do you want me to phone Peggy?" I said. Peggy is my sister. She is married to an astronomer and lives in Victoria.

He thought about it. "I guess we ought to tell them," he said finally. "But tell them not to get alarmed."

"All right."

"No, wait a minute. Sam is supposed to be going to a con-ference the end of this week, and Peggy was planning to go along with him. I don't want them wondering about changing their plans."

"Where is the conference?"

"Amsterdam," he said proudly. He did take pride in Sam, and kept track of his books and articles. He would pick one up and say, "Look at that, will you? And I can't understand a word of it!" in a marvelling voice that managed nevertheless to have a trace of ridicule.

"Professor Sam," he would say. "And the three little Sams." This is what he called his grandsons, who did resemble their father in braininess and in almost endearing pushiness—an innocent energetic showing-off. They went to a private school that favored old-fashioned discipline and started calculus in Grade 5. "And the dogs," he might enumerate further, "who have been to obedience school. And Peggy . . ."

But if I said, "Do you suppose she has been to obedience school, too?" he would play the game no further. I imagine that when he was with Sam and Peggy he spoke of me in the same way—hinted at my flightiness just as he hinted at their stodginess, made mild jokes at my expense, did not quite con-ceal his amazement (or pretended not to conceal his amaze-ment) that people paid money for things I had written. He had to do this so that he might never seem to brag, but he would put up the gates when the joking got too rough. And of course I found later, in the house, things of mine he had kept—a few magazines, clippings, things I had never bothered about.

Now his thoughts travelled from Peggy's family to mine. "Have you heard from Judith?" he said.

"Not yet."

"Well, it's pretty soon. Were they going to sleep in the van?"

"Yes."

"I guess it's safe enough, if they stop in the right places."

I knew he would have to say something more and I knew it would come as a joke.

"I guess they put a board down the middle, like the pioneers?"

I smiled but did not answer.

"I take it you have no objections?"

"No," I said.

"Well, I always believed that, too. Keep out of your children's business. I tried not to say anything. I never said anything when you left Richard."

"What do you mean, 'said anything'? Criticize?"

"It wasn't any of my business."

"No."

"But that doesn't mean I was pleased."

I was surprised—not just at what he said but at his feeling that he had any right, even now, to say it. I had to look out the window and down at the traffic to control myself.

"I just wanted you to know," he added.

A long time ago, he said to me in his mild way, "It's funny. Richard when I first saw him reminded me of what my father used to say. He'd say if that fellow was half as smart as he thinks he is, he'd be twice as smart as he really is."

I turned to remind him of this, but found myself looking at the line his heart was writing. Not that there seemed to be anything wrong, any difference in the beeps and points. But it was there.

He saw where I was looking. "Unfair advantage," he said.

"It is," I said. "I'm going to have to get hooked up, too."

We laughed, we kissed formally; I left. At least he hadn't asked me about Nichola, I thought.

The next afternoon I didn't go to the hospital, because my father was having some more tests done, to prepare for the operation. I was to see him in the evening instead. I found myself wandering through the Bloor Street dress shops, trying on clothes. A preoccupation with fashion and my own appearance had descended on me like a raging headache. I looked at the women in the street, at the clothes in the shops, trying to discover how a transformation might be made, what I would have to buy. I recognized this obsession for what it was but had trouble shaking it. I've had people tell me that waiting for life-or-death news they've stood in front of an open refrigerator eating anything in sight—cold boiled potatoes, chili sauce, bowls of whipped cream. Or have been unable to stop doing crossword puzzles. Attention narrows in on something—some distraction—grabs on, becomes fanatically serious. I shuffled clothes on the racks, pulled them on in hot little changing rooms in front of cruel mirrors. I was sweating; once or twice I thought I might faint. Out on the street again, I thought I must remove myself from Bloor Street, and decided to go to the museum.

I remembered another time, in Vancouver. It was when Nichola was going to kindergarten and Judith was a baby. Nichola had been to the doctor about a cold, or maybe for a routine examination, and the blood test revealed something about her white blood cells—either that there were too many of them or that they were enlarged. The doctor ordered further tests, and I took Nichola to the hospital for them. Nobody mentioned leukemia but I knew, of course, what they were looking for. When I took Nichola home I asked the baby-sitter who had been with Judith to stay for the afternoon and I went shopping. I bought the most daring dress I ever owned, a black silk sheath with some laced-up arrangement in front. I remembered that bright spring afternoon, the spike-heeled shoes in the department store, the underwear printed with leopard spots.

I also remembered going home from St. Paul's Hospital over the Lions Gate Bridge on the crowded bus and holding Nichola on my knee. She suddenly recalled her baby name for bridge and whispered to me, "Whee—over the whee." I did not avoid touching my child—Nichola was slender and graceful even then, with a pretty back and fine dark hair—but realized I was touching her with a difference, though I did not think it could ever be detected. There was care—not a withdrawal exactly but a care—not to feel anything much. I saw how the forms of love might be maintained with a condemned person but with the love in fact measured and disciplined, because you have to survive. It could be done so discreetly that the object of such care would not suspect, any more than she would suspect the sentence of death itself. Nichola did not know, would not know. Toys and kisses and jokes would come tumbling over her; she would never know, though I worried that she would feel the wind between the cracks of the manufactured holidays, the manufactured normal days. But all was well. Nichola did not have leukemia. She grew up—was still alive, and possibly happy. Incommunicado.

I could not think of anything in the museum I really wanted to see, so I walked past it to the planetarium. I had never been to a planetarium. The show was due to start in ten minutes. I went inside, bought a ticket, got in line. There was a whole class of schoolchildren, maybe a couple of classes, with teachers and volunteer mothers riding herd on them. I looked around to see if there were any other unattached adults. Only one—a man with a red face and puffy eyes, who looked as if he might be here to keep himself from going to a bar.

Inside, we sat on wonderfully comfortable seats that were tilted back so that you lay in a sort of hammock, attention directed to the bowl of the ceiling, which soon turned dark blue, with a faint rim of light all around the edge. There was some splendid, commanding music. The adults all around were shushing the children, trying to make them stop crackling their potato-chip bags. Then a man's voice, an eloquent professional voice, began to speak slowly, out of the walls. The voice reminded me a little of the way radio announcers used to introduce a piece of classical music or describe the progress of the Royal Family to Westminster Abbey on one of their royal occasions. There was a faint echo-chamber effect.

The dark ceiling was filling with stars. They came out not all at once but one after another, the way the stars really do come out at night, though more quickly. The Milky Way appeared, was moving closer; stars swam into brilliance and kept on going, disappearing beyond the edges of the sky-screen or behind my head. While the flow of light continued, the voice presented the stunning facts. A few light-years away, it announced, the sun appears as a bright star, and the planets are not visible. A few dozen light-years away, the sun is not visible, either, to the naked eye. And that distance—a few dozen light-years—is only about a thousandth part of the distance from the sun to the center of our galaxy, one galaxy, which itself contains about two hundred billion suns. And is, in turn, one of millions, perhaps billions, of galaxies. Innumerable repetitions, innumerable variations. All this rolled past my head, too, like balls of lightning.

Now realism was abandoned, for familiar artifice. A model of the solar system was spinning away in its elegant style. A bright bug took off from the earth, heading for Jupiter. I set my dodging and shrinking mind sternly to recording facts. The mass of Jupiter two and a half times that of all the other planets put together. The Great Red Spot. The thirteen moons. Past Jupiter, a glance at the eccentric orbit of Pluto, the icy rings of Saturn. Back to Earth and moving in to hot and dazzling Venus. Atmospheric pressure ninety times ours. Moonless Mercury rotating three times while circling the sun twice; an odd arrangement, not as satisfying as what they used to tell us—that it rotated once as it circled the sun. No perpetual darkness after all. Why did they give out such confident information, only to announce later that it was quite wrong? Finally, the picture already familiar from magazines: the red soil of Mars, the blooming pink sky.

When the show was over I sat in my seat while the children clambered across me, making no comments on anything they had just seen or heard. They were pestering their keepers for eatables and further entertainments. An effort had been made to get their attention, to take it away from canned pop and potato chips and fix it on various knowns and unknowns and horrible immensities, and it seemed to have failed. A good thing, too, I thought. Children have a natural immunity, most of them, and it shouldn't be tampered with. As for the adults who would deplore it, the ones who promoted this show, weren't they immune themselves to the extent that they could put in the echo-chamber effects, the music, the churchlike solemnity, simulating the awe that they supposed they ought to feel? Awe—what was that supposed to be? A fit of the shivers when you looked out the window? Once you knew what it was, you wouldn't be courting it.

Two men came with brooms to sweep up the debris the audience had left behind. They told me that the next show would start in forty minutes. In the meantime, I had to get out.

"I went to the show at the planetarium," I said to my father. "It was very exciting—about the solar system." I thought what a silly word I had used: "exciting." "It's like a slightly phony temple," I added.

He was already talking. "I remember when they found Pluto. Right where they thought it had to be. Mercury, Venus, Earth, Mars," he recited. "Jupiter, Saturn, Nept—no, Uranus, Neptune, Pluto. Is that right?"

"Yes," I said. I was just as glad he hadn't heard what I said about the phony temple. I had meant that to be truthful, but it sounded slick and superior. "Tell me the moons of Jupiter."

"Well, I don't know the new ones. There's a bunch of new ones, isn't there?"

"Two. But they're not new."

"New to us," said my father. "You've turned pretty cheeky now I'm going under the knife."

"'Under the knife.' What an expression."

He was not in bed tonight, his last night. He had been detached from his apparatus, and was sitting in a chair by the window. He was bare-legged, wearing a hospital dressing gown, but he did not look self-conscious or out of place. He looked thoughtful but good-humored, an affable host.

"You haven't even named the old ones," I said.

"Give me time. Galileo named them. Io."

"That's a start."

"The moons of Jupiter were the first heavenly bodies discovered with the telescope." He said this gravely, as if he could see the sentence in an old book. "It wasn't Galileo named them, either; it was some German. Io, Europa, Ganymede, Callisto. There you are."

"Yes."

"Io and Europa, they were girlfriends of Jupiter's, weren't they? Ganymede was a boy. A shepherd? I don't know who Callisto was."

"I think she was a girlfriend, too," I said. "Jupiter's wife—Jove's wife—changed her into a bear and stuck her up in the sky. Great Bear and Little Bear. Little Bear was her baby."

The loudspeaker said that it was time for visitors to go.

"I'll see you when you come out of the anesthetic," I said.

"Yes."

When I was at the door, he called to me, "Ganymede wasn't any shepherd. He was Jove's cupbearer."

When I left the planetarium that afternoon, I had walked through the museum to the Chinese garden. I saw the stone camels again, the warriors, the tomb. I sat on a bench looking toward Bloor Street. Through the evergreen bushes and the high grilled iron fence I watched people going by in the late-afternoon sunlight. The planetarium show had done what I wanted it to after all—calmed me down, drained me. I saw a girl who reminded me of Nichola. She wore a trenchcoat and carried a bag of groceries. She was shorter than Nichola—not really much like her at all—but I thought that I might see Nichola. She would be walking along some street maybe not far from here—burdened, preoccupied, alone. She was one of the grownup people in the world now, one of the shoppers going home.

If I did see her, I might just sit and watch, I decided. I felt like one of those people who have floated up to the ceiling, enjoying a brief death. A relief, while it lasts. My father had chosen and Nichola had chosen. Someday, probably soon, I would hear from her, but it came to the same thing.

I meant to get up and go over to the tomb, to look at the relief carvings, the stone pictures, that go all the way around it. I always mean to look at them and I never do. Not this time, either. It was getting cold out, so I went inside to have coffee and something to eat before I went back to the hospital.

THE PROGRESS
OF LOVE

I got a call at work, and it was my father. This was not long
after I was divorced and started in the real-estate office. Both of
my boys were in school. It was a hot enough day in September.
My father was so polite, even in the family. He took time to
ask me how I was. Country manners. Even if somebody
phones up to tell you your house is burning down, they ask
first how you are.

"I'm fine," I said. "How are you?"

"Not so good, I guess," said my father, in his old way—
apologetic but self-respecting. "I think your mother's gone."

I knew that "gone" meant "dead." I knew that. But for a second or so I saw my mother in her black straw hat setting off
down the lane. The word "gone" seemed full of nothing but a
deep relief and even an excitement—the excitement you feel
when a door closes and your house sinks back to normal and you
let yourself loose into all the free space around you. That was in
my father's voice, too—behind the apology, a queer sound like a
gulped breath. But my mother hadn't been a burden—she hadn't
been sick a day—and far from feeling relieved at her death, my

father took it hard. He never got used to living alone, he said. He went into the Netterfield County Home quite willingly.

He told me how he found my mother on the couch in the kitchen when he came in at noon. She had picked a few tomatoes, and was setting them on the windowsill to ripen; then she must have felt weak, and lain down. Now, telling this, his voice went wobbly—meandering, as you would expect—in his amazement. I saw in my mind the couch, the old quilt that protected it, right under the phone.

"So I thought I better call you," my father said, and he waited for me to say what he should do now.

My mother prayed on her knees at midday, at night, and first thing in the morning. Every day opened up to her to have God's will done in it. Every night she totted up what she'd done and said and thought, to see how it squared with Him. That kind of life is dreary, people think, but they're missing the point. For one thing, such a life can never be boring. And nothing can happen to you that you can't make use of. Even if you're racked by troubles, and sick and poor and ugly, you've got your soul to carry through life like a treasure on a platter. Going upstairs to pray after the noon meal, my mother would be full of energy and expectation, seriously smiling.

She was saved at a camp meeting when she was fourteen. That was the same summer that her own mother—my grandmother—died. For a few years, my mother went to meetings with a lot of other people who'd been saved, some who'd been saved over and over again, enthusiastic old sinners. She could tell stories about what went on at those meetings, the singing and hollering and wildness. She told about one old man getting up and shouting, "Come down, O Lord, come down

among us now! Come down through the roof and I'll pay for
the shingles!"

She was back to being just an Anglican, a serious one, by the
time she got married. She was twenty-five then, and my father
was thirty-eight. A tall good-looking couple, good dancers,
good cardplayers, sociable. But serious people—that's how I
would try to describe them. Serious the way hardly anybody is
anymore. My father was not religious in the way my mother
was. He was an Anglican, an Orangeman, a Conservative,
because that's what he had been brought up to be. He was the
son who got left on the farm with his parents and took care of
them till they died. He met my mother, he waited for her, they
married; he thought himself lucky then to have a family to work
for. (I have two brothers, and I had a baby sister who died.) I
have a feeling that my father never slept with any woman before
my mother, and never with her until he married her. And he
had to wait, because my mother wouldn't get married until she
had paid back to her own father every cent he had spent on her
since her mother died. She had kept track of everything—board,
books, clothes—so that she could pay it back. When she married, she had no nest egg, as teachers usually did, no hope chest,
sheets, or dishes. My father used to say, with a somber, joking
face, that he had hoped to get a woman with money in the bank.
"But you take the money in the bank, you have to take the face
that goes with it," he said, "and sometimes that's no bargain."

The house we lived in had big, high rooms, with dark-green
blinds on the windows. When the blinds were pulled down
against the sun, I used to like to move my head and catch the
light flashing through the holes and cracks. Another thing I
liked looking at was chimney stains, old or fresh, which I could
turn into animals, people's faces, even distant cities. I told my

own two boys about that, and their father, Dan Casey, said, "See, your mom's folks were so poor, they couldn't afford TV, so they got these stains on the ceiling—your mom had to watch the stains on the ceiling!" He always liked to kid me about thinking poor was anything great.

When my father was very old, I figured out that he didn't mind people doing new sorts of things—for instance, my getting divorced—as much as he minded them having new sorts of reasons for doing them.

Thank God he never had to know about the commune.

"The Lord never intended," he used to say. Sitting around with the other old men in the Home, in the long, dim porch behind the spirea bushes, he talked about how the Lord never intended for people to tear around the country on motorbikes and snowmobiles. And how the Lord never intended for nurses' uniforms to be pants. The nurses didn't mind at all. They called him "Handsome," and told me he was a real old sweetheart, a real old religious gentleman. They marvelled at his thick black hair, which he kept until he died. They washed and combed it beautifully, wet-waved it with their fingers.

Sometimes, with all their care, he was a little unhappy. He wanted to go home. He worried about the cows, the fences, about who was getting up to light the fire. A few flashes of meanness—very few. Once, he gave me a sneaky, unfriendly look when I went in; he said, "I'm surprised you haven't worn all the skin off your knees by now."

I laughed. I said. "What doing? Scrubbing floors?"

"Praying!" he said, in a voice like spitting.

He didn't know who he was talking to.

———

I don't remember my mother's hair being anything but white. My mother went white in her twenties, and never saved any of her young hair, which had been brown. I used to try to get her to tell what color brown.

"Dark."

"Like Brent, or like Dolly?" Those were two workhorses we had, a team.

"I don't know. It wasn't horsehair."

"Was it like chocolate?"

"Something like."

"Weren't you sad when it went white?"

"No. I was glad."

"Why?"

"I was glad that I wouldn't have hair anymore that was the same color as my father's."

Hatred is always a sin, my mother told me. Remember that. One drop of hatred in your soul will spread and discolor everything like a drop of black ink in white milk. I was struck by that and meant to try it, but knew I shouldn't waste the milk.

All these things I remember. All the things I know, or have been told, about people I never even saw. I was named Euphemia, after my mother's mother. A terrible name, such as nobody has nowadays. At home they called me Phemie, but when I started to work, I called myself Fame. My husband, Dan Casey, called me Fame. Then in the bar of the Shamrock Hotel, years later, after my divorce, when I was going out, a man said to me, "Fame, I've been meaning to ask you, just what is it you are famous for?"

"I don't know," I told him. "I don't know, unless it's for wasting my time talking to jerks like you."

After that I thought of changing it altogether, to something like Joan, but unless I moved away from here, how could I do that?

In the summer of 1947, when I was twelve, I helped my mother paper the downstairs bedroom, the spare room. My mother's sister, Beryl, was coming to visit us. These two sisters hadn't seen each other for years. Very soon after their mother died, their father married again. He went to live in Minneapolis, then in Seattle, with his new wife and his younger daughter, Beryl. My mother wouldn't go with them. She stayed on in the town of Ramsay, where they had been living. She was boarded with a childless couple who had been neighbors. She and Beryl had met only once or twice since they were grown up. Beryl lived in California.

The paper had a design of cornflowers on a white ground. My mother had got it at a reduced price, because it was the end of a lot. This meant we had trouble matching the pattern, and behind the door we had to do some tricky fitting with scraps and strips. This was before the days of pre-pasted wallpaper. We had a trestle table set up in the front room, and we mixed the paste and swept it onto the back of the paper with wide brushes, watching for lumps. We worked with the windows up, screens fitted under them, the front door open, the screen door closed. The country we could see through the mesh of screens and the wavery old window glass was all hot and flowering—milkweed and wild carrot in the pastures, mustard rampaging in the clover, some fields creamy with the buckwheat people grew then. My mother sang. She sang a song she said her own mother used to sing when she and Beryl were little girls.

"I once had a sweetheart, but now I have none.
He's gone and he's left me to weep and to moan.

He's gone and he's left me, but contented I'll be,
For I'll get another one, better than he!"

I was excited because Beryl was coming, a visitor, all the way
from California. Also, because I had gone to town in late June
to write the Entrance Examinations, and was hoping to hear
soon that I had passed with honors. Everybody who had finished Grade 8 in the country schools had to go into town to
write those examinations. I loved that—the rustling sheets of
foolscap, the important silence, the big stone high-school
building, all the old initials carved in the desks, darkened with
varnish. The first burst of summer outside, the green and yellow light, the townlike chestnut trees, and honeysuckle. And all
it was was this same town, where I have lived now more than
half my life. I wondered at it. And at myself, drawing maps
with ease and solving problems, knowing quantities of answers.
I thought I was so clever. But I wasn't clever enough to understand the simplest thing. I didn't even understand that examinations made no difference in my case. I wouldn't be going to
high school. How could I? That was before there were school
buses; you had to board in town. My parents didn't have the
money. They operated on very little cash, as many farmers did
then. The payments from the cheese factory were about all that
came in regularly. And they didn't think of my life going in
that direction, the high-school direction. They thought that I
would stay at home and help my mother, maybe hire out to
help women in the neighborhood who were sick or having a
baby. Until such time as I got married. That was what they were
waiting to tell me when I got the results of the examinations.

You would think my mother might have a different idea,
since she had been a schoolteacher herself. But she said God
didn't care. God isn't interested in what kind of job or what

kind of education anybody has, she told me. He doesn't care two hoots about that, and it's what He cares about that matters.

This was the first time I understood how God could become a real opponent, not just some kind of nuisance or large decoration.

My mother's name as a child was Marietta. That continued to be her name, of course, but until Beryl came I never heard her called by it. My father always said Mother. I had a childish notion—I knew it was childish—that Mother suited my mother better than it did other mothers. Mother, not Mama. When I was away from her, I could not think what my mother's face was like, and this frightened me. Sitting in school, just over a hill from home, I would try to picture my mother's face. Sometimes I thought that if I couldn't do it, that might mean my mother was dead. But I had a sense of her all the time, and would be reminded of her by the most unlikely things—an upright piano, or a tall white loaf of bread. That's ridiculous, but true.

Marietta, in my mind, was separate, not swallowed up in my mother's grownup body. Marietta was still running around loose up in her town of Ramsay, on the Ottawa River. In that town, the streets were full of horses and puddles, and darkened by men who came in from the bush on weekends. Loggers. There were eleven hotels on the main street, where the loggers stayed, and drank.

The house Marietta lived in was halfway up a steep street climbing from the river. It was a double house, with two bay windows in front, and a wooden trellis that separated the two front porches. In the other half of the house lived the Sutcliffes, the people Marietta was to board with after her mother died and her father left town. Mr. Sutcliffe was an Englishman, a telegraph operator. His wife was German. She always made coffee instead of tea. She made strudel. The dough for the strudel hung down over the edges of the table like a fine cloth. It sometimes looked to Marietta like a skin. Mrs. Sutcliffe was the one who talked Marietta's mother out of hanging herself.

Marietta was home from school that day, because it was Saturday. She woke up late and heard the silence in the house. She was always scared of that—a silent house—and as soon as she opened the door after school she would call, "Mama! Mama!" Often her mother wouldn't answer. But she would be there. Marietta would hear with relief the rattle of the stove grate or the steady slap of the iron.

That morning, she didn't hear anything. She came downstairs, and got herself a slice of bread and butter and molasses, folded over. She opened the cellar door and called. She went into the front room and peered out the window, through the bridal fern. She saw her little sister, Beryl, and some other neighborhood children rolling down the bit of grassy terrace to the sidewalk, picking themselves up and scrambling to the top and rolling down again.

"Mama?" called Marietta. She walked through the house to the backyard. It was late spring, the day was cloudy and mild. In the sprouting vegetable gardens, the earth was damp, and the leaves on the trees seemed suddenly full-sized, letting down drops of water left over from the rain of the night before.

"Mama?" called Marietta under the trees, under the clothesline.

At the end of the yard is a small barn, where they keep firewood, and some tools and old furniture. A chair, a straight-backed wooden chair, can be seen through the open doorway. On the chair, Marietta sees her mother's feet, her mother's black laced shoes. Then the long, printed cotton summer work dress, the apron, the rolled-up sleeves. Her mother's shiny-looking white arms, and neck, and face.

Her mother stood on the chair and didn't answer. She didn't look at Marietta, but smiled and tapped her foot, as if to say, "Here I am, then. What are you going to do about it?" Something looked wrong about her, beyond the fact that she was standing on a chair and smiling in this queer, tight way. Standing on an old chair with back rungs missing, which she had pulled out to the middle of the barn floor, where it teetered on the bumpy earth. There was a shadow on her neck.

The shadow was a rope, a noose on the end of a rope that hung down from a beam overhead.

"Mama?" says Marietta, in a fainter voice. "Mama. Come down, please." Her voice is faint because she fears that any yell or cry might jolt her mother into movement, cause her to step off the chair and throw her weight on the rope. But even if Marietta wanted to yell she couldn't. Nothing but this pitiful thread of a voice is left to her—just as in a dream when a beast or a machine is bearing down on you.

"Go and get your father."

That was what her mother told her to do, and Marietta obeyed. With terror in her legs, she ran. In her nightgown, in the middle of a Saturday morning, she ran. She ran past Beryl and the other children, still tumbling down the slope. She ran along the sidewalk, which was at that time a boardwalk, then on the unpaved street, full of last night's puddles. The street crossed the railway tracks. At the foot of the hill, it intersected the main street of the town. Between the main street and the river were some warehouses and the buildings of small manufacturers. That was where Marietta's father had his carriage works. Wagons, buggies, sleds were made there. In fact, Marietta's father had invented a new sort of sled to carry logs in the bush. It had been patented. He was just getting started in Ramsay. (Later on, in the States, he made money. A man fond of hotel bars, barbershops, harness races, women, but not afraid of work—give him credit.)

Marietta did not find him at work that day. The office was empty. She ran out into the yard where the men were working. She stumbled in the fresh sawdust. The men laughed and shook their heads at her. No. Not here. Not a-here right now. No. Why don't you try upstreet? Wait. Wait a minute. Hadn't you better get some clothes on first?

They didn't mean any harm. They didn't have the sense to see that something must be wrong. But Marietta never could stand men laughing. There were always places she hated to go past, let alone into, and that was the reason. Men laughing. Because of that, she hated barbershops, hated their smell. (When she started going to dances later on with my father, she asked him not to put any dressing on his hair, because the smell reminded her.) A bunch of men standing out on the street, outside a hotel, seemed to Marietta like a clot of poison. You tried not to hear what they were saying, but you could be sure it was vile. If they didn't say anything, they laughed and vileness spread out from them—poison—just the same. It was only after Marietta was saved that she could walk right past them. Armed by God, she walked through their midst and nothing stuck to her, nothing scorched her; she was safe as Daniel.

Now she turned and ran, straight back the way she had come. Up the hill, running to get home. She thought she had made a mistake leaving her mother. Why did her mother tell her to go? Why did she want her father? Quite possibly so that she could greet him with the sight of her own warm body swinging on the end of a rope. Marietta should have stayed—she should have stayed and talked her mother out of it. She should have run to Mrs. Sutcliffe, or any neighbor, not wasted time this way. She hadn't thought who could help, who could even believe what she was talking about. She had the idea that all families except her own lived in peace, that threats and miseries didn't exist in other people's houses, and couldn't be explained there.

A train was coming into town. Marietta had to wait. Passengers looked out at her from its windows. She broke out wailing in the faces of those strangers. When the train passed, she continued up the hill—a spectacle, with her hair uncombed, her feet bare and muddy, in her nightgown, with a wild, wet face. By the time she ran into her own yard, in sight of the barn, she was howling. "Mama!" she was howling. "Mama!"

Nobody was there. The chair was standing just where it had been before. The rope was dangling over the back of it. Marietta was sure that her mother had gone ahead and done it. Her mother was already dead—she had been cut down and taken away.

But warm, fat hands settled down on her shoulders, and Mrs. Sutcliffe said, "Marietta. Stop the noise. Marietta. Child. Stop the crying. Come inside. She is well, Marietta. Come inside and you will see."

Mrs. Sutcliffe's foreign voice said, "Mari-et-cha," giving the name a rich, important sound. She was as kind as could be. When Marietta lived with the Sutcliffes later, she was treated as the daughter of the household, and it was a household just as peaceful and comfortable as she had imagined other households to be. But she never felt like a daughter there.

In Mrs. Sutcliffe's kitchen, Beryl sat on the floor eating a raisin cookie and playing with the black-and-white cat, whose name was Dickie. Marietta's mother sat at the table, with a cup of coffee in front of her.

"She was silly," Mrs. Sutcliffe said. Did she mean Marietta's mother or Marietta herself? She didn't have many English words to describe things.

Marietta's mother laughed, and Marietta blacked out. She fainted, after running all that way uphill, howling, in the warm, damp morning. Next thing she knew, she was taking black, sweet coffee from a spoon held by Mrs. Sutcliffe. Beryl picked Dickie up by the front legs and offered him as a cheering present. Marietta's mother was still sitting at the table.

Her heart was broken. That was what I always heard my mother say. That was the end of it. Those words lifted up the story and sealed it shut. I never asked, Who broke it? I never asked, What was the men's poison talk? What was the meaning of the word "vile"?

Marietta's mother laughed after not hanging herself. She sat at Mrs. Sutcliffe's kitchen table long ago and laughed. Her heart was broken.

I always had a feeling, with my mother's talk and stories, of something swelling out behind. Like a cloud you couldn't see through, or get to the end of. There was a cloud, a poison, that had touched my mother's life. And when I grieved my mother, I became part of it. Then I would beat my head against my mother's stomach and breasts, against her tall, firm front, demanding to be forgiven. My mother would tell me to ask God. But it wasn't God, it was my mother I had to get straight with. It seemed as if she knew something about me that was worse, far worse, than ordinary lies and tricks and meanness; it was a really sickening shame. I beat against my mother's front to make her forget that.

My brothers weren't bothered by any of this. I don't think so. They seemed to me like cheerful savages, running around free, not having to learn much. And when I just had the two boys myself, no daughters, I felt as if something could stop now—the stories, and griefs, the old puzzles you can't resist or solve.

Aunt Beryl said not to call her Aunt. "I'm not used to being anybody's aunt, honey. I'm not even anybody's momma. I'm just me. Call me Beryl."

Beryl had started out as a stenographer, and now she had her own typing and bookkeeping business, which employed many girls. She had arrived with a man friend, whose name was Mr. Florence. Her letter had said that she would be getting a ride with a friend, but she hadn't said whether the friend would be staying or going on. She hadn't even said if it was a man or a woman.

Mr. Florence was staying. He was a tall, thin man with a long, tanned face, very light-colored eyes, and a way of twitching the corner of his mouth that might have been a smile.

He was the one who got to sleep in the room that my mother and I had papered, because he was the stranger, and a man. Beryl had to sleep with me. At first we thought that Mr. Florence was quite rude, because he wasn't used to our way of talking and we weren't used to his. The first morning, my father said to Mr. Florence, "Well, I hope you got some kind of sleep on that old bed in there?" (The spare-room bed was heavenly, with a feather tick.) This was Mr. Florence's cue to say that he had never slept better.

Mr. Florence twitched. He said, "I slept on worse."

His favorite place to be was in his car. His car was a royal-blue Chrysler, from the first batch turned out after the war. Inside it, the upholstery and floor covering and roof and door padding were all pearl gray. Mr. Florence kept the names of those colors in mind and corrected you if you said just "blue" or "gray."

"Mouse skin is what it looks like to me," said Beryl rambunctiously. "I tell him it's just mouse skin!"

The car was parked at the side of the house, under the locust trees. Mr. Florence sat inside with the windows rolled up, smoking, in the rich new-car smell.

"I'm afraid we're not doing much to entertain your friend," my mother said.

"I wouldn't worry about him," said Beryl. She always spoke about Mr. Florence as if there was a joke about him that only she appreciated. I wondered long afterward if he had a bottle in the glove compartment and took a nip from time to time to keep his spirits up. He kept his hat on.

Beryl herself was being entertained enough for two. Instead of staying in the house and talking to my mother, as a lady visitor usually did, she demanded to be shown everything there was to see on a farm. She said that I was to take her around and explain things, and see that she didn't fall into any manure piles.

I didn't know what to show. I took Beryl to the icehouse, where chunks of ice the size of dresser drawers, or bigger, lay buried in sawdust. Every few days, my father would chop off a piece of ice and carry it to the kitchen, where it melted in a tin-lined box and cooled the milk and butter.

Beryl said she had never had any idea ice came in pieces that big. She seemed intent on finding things strange, or horrible, or funny.

"Where in the world do you get ice that big?"

I couldn't tell if that was a joke.

"Off of the lake," I said.

"Off of the lake! Do you have lakes up here that have ice on them all summer?"

I told her how my father cut the ice on the lake every winter and hauled it home, and buried it in sawdust, and that kept it from melting.

Beryl said, "That's amazing!"

"Well, it melts a little," I said. I was deeply disappointed in Beryl.

"That's really amazing."

Beryl went along when I went to get the cows. A scarecrow in white slacks (this was what my father called her afterward), with a white sun hat tied under her chin by a flaunting red ribbon. Her fingernails and toenails—she wore sandals—were painted to match the ribbon. She wore the small, dark sunglasses people wore at that time. (Not the people I knew—they didn't own sunglasses.) She had a big red mouth, a loud laugh, hair of an unnatural color and a high gloss, like cherry wood. She was so noisy and shiny, so glamorously got up, that it was hard to tell whether she was good-looking, or happy, or anything.

We didn't have any conversation along the cowpath, because Beryl kept her distance from the cows and was busy watching where she stepped. Once I had them all tied in their stalls, she came closer. She lit a cigarette. Nobody smoked in the barn. My father and other farmers chewed tobacco there instead. I didn't see how I could ask Beryl to chew tobacco.

"Can you get the milk out of them or does your father have to?" Beryl said. "Is it hard to do?"

I pulled some milk down through the cow's teat. One of the barn cats came over and waited. I shot a thin stream into its mouth. The cat and I were both showing off.

"Doesn't that hurt?" said Beryl. "Think if it was you."

I had never thought of a cow's teat as corresponding to any part of myself, and was shaken by this indecency. In fact, I could never grasp a warm, warty teat in such a firm and casual way again.

Beryl slept in a peach-colored rayon nightgown trimmed with écru lace. She had a robe to match. She was just as careful about the word "écru" as Mr. Florence was about his royal blue and pearl gray. I managed to get undressed and put on my nightgown without any part of me being exposed at any time. An awkward business. I left my underpants on, and hoped that Beryl had done the same. The idea of sharing my bed with a grownup was a torment to me. But I did get to see the contents of what Beryl called her beauty kit. Hand-painted glass jars contained puffs of cotton wool, talcum powder, milky lotion, ice-blue astringent. Little pots of red and mauve rouge—rather greasy-looking. Blue and black pencils. Emery boards, a pumice stone, nail polish with an overpowering smell of bananas, face powder in a celluloid box shaped like a shell, with the name of a dessert—Apricot Delight.

I had heated some water on the coal-oil stove we used in summertime. Beryl scrubbed her face clean, and there was such a change that I almost expected to see makeup lying in strips in the washbowl, like the old wallpaper we had soaked and peeled. Beryl's skin was pale now, covered with fine cracks, rather like the shiny mud at the bottom of puddles drying up in early summer.

"Look what happened to my skin," she said. "Dieting. I weighed a hundred and sixty-nine pounds once, and I took it off too fast and my face fell in on me. Now I've got this cream, though. It's made from a secret formula and you can't even buy it commercially. Smell it. See, it doesn't smell all perfumy. It smells serious."

She was patting the cream on her face with puffs of cotton

wool, patting away until there was nothing to be seen on the surface.

"It smells like lard," I said.

"Christ Almighty, I hope I haven't been paying that kind of money to rub lard on my face. Don't tell your mother I swear."

She poured clean water into the drinking glass and wet her comb, then combed her hair wet and twisted each strand round her finger, clamping the twisted strand to her head with two crossed pins. I would be doing the same myself, a couple of years later.

"Always do your hair wet, else it's no good doing it up at all," Beryl said. "And always roll it under even if you want it to flip up. See?"

When I was doing my hair up—as I did for years—I sometimes thought of this, and thought that of all the pieces of advice people had given me, this was the one I had followed most carefully.

We put the lamp out and got into bed, and Beryl said, "I never knew it could get so dark. I've never known a dark that was as dark as this." She was whispering. I was slow to understand that she was comparing country nights to city nights, and I wondered if the darkness in Netterfield County could really be greater than that in California.

"Honey?" whispered Beryl. "Are there any animals outside?"

"Cows," I said.

"Yes, but wild animals? Are there bears?"

"Yes," I said. My father had once found bear tracks and droppings in the bush, and the apples had all been torn off a wild apple tree. That was years ago, when he was a young man.

Beryl moaned and giggled. "Think if Mr. Florence had to go out in the night and he ran into a bear!"

Next day was Sunday. Beryl and Mr. Florence drove my brothers and me to Sunday school in the Chrysler. That was at ten o'clock in the morning. They came back at eleven to bring my parents to church.

"Hop in," Beryl said to me. "You, too," she said to the boys. "We're going for a drive."

Beryl was dressed up in a satiny ivory dress with red dots, and a red-lined frill over the hips, and red high-heeled shoes. Mr. Florence wore a pale-blue summer suit.

"Aren't you going to church?" I said. That was what people dressed up for, in my experience.

Beryl laughed. "Honey, this isn't Mr. Florence's kind of religion."

I was used to going straight from Sunday school into church, and sitting for another hour and a half. In summer, the open windows let in the cedary smell of the graveyard and the occasional, almost sacrilegious sound of a car swooshing by on the road. Today we spent this time driving through country I had never seen before. I had never seen it, though it was less than twenty miles from home. Our truck went to the cheese factory, to church, and to town on Saturday nights. The nearest thing to a drive was when it went to the dump. I had seen the near end of Bell's Lake, because that was where my father cut the ice in winter. You couldn't get close to it in summer; the shoreline was all choked up with bulrushes. I had thought that the other end of the lake would look pretty much the same, but when we drove there today, I saw cottages, docks and boats, dark water reflecting the trees. All this and I hadn't know about it. This, too, was Bell's Lake. I was glad to have seen it at last, but in some way not altogether glad of the surprise.

Finally, a white frame building appeared, with verandas and

potted flowers, and some twinkling poplar trees in front. The Wildwood Inn. Today the same building is covered with stucco and done up with Tudor beams and called the Hideaway. The poplar trees have been cut down for a parking lot.

On the way back to the church to pick up my parents, Mr. Florence turned in to the farm next to ours, which belonged to the McAllisters. The McAllisters were Catholics. Our two families were neighborly but not close.

"Come on, boys, out you get," said Beryl to my brothers. "Not you," she said to me. "You stay put." She herded the little boys up to the porch, where some McAllisters were watching. They were in their raggedy home clothes, because their church, or Mass, or whatever it was, got out early. Mrs. McAllister came out and stood listening, rather dumbfounded, to Beryl's laughing talk.

Beryl came back to the car by herself. "There," she said. "They're going to play with the neighbor children."

Play with McAllisters? Besides being Catholics, all but the baby were girls.

"They've still got their good clothes on," I said.

"So what? Can't they have a good time with their good clothes on? I do!"

My parents were taken by surprise as well. Beryl got out and told my father he was to ride in the front seat, for the legroom. She got into the back, with my mother and me. Mr. Florence turned again onto the Bell's Lake road, and Beryl announced that we were all going to the Wildwood Inn for dinner.

"You're all dressed up, why not take advantage?" she said. "We dropped the boys off with your neighbors. I thought they might be too young to appreciate it. The neighbors were happy to have them." She said with a further emphasis that it was to be their treat. Hers and Mr. Florence's.

"Well, now," said my father. He probably didn't have five

dollars in his pocket. "Well, now. I wonder do they let the farmers in?"

He made various jokes along this line. In the hotel dining room, which was all in white—white tablecloths, white painted chairs—with sweating glass water pitchers and high, whirring fans, he picked up a table napkin the size of a diaper and spoke to me in a loud whisper, "Can you tell me what to do with this thing? Can I put it on my head to keep the draft off?"

Of course he had eaten in hotel dining rooms before. He knew about table napkins and pie forks. And my mother knew—she wasn't even a country woman, to begin with. Nevertheless this was a huge event. Not exactly a pleasure—as Beryl must have meant it to be—but a huge, unsettling event. Eating a meal in public, only a few miles from home, eating in a big room full of people you didn't know, the food served by a stranger, a snippy-looking girl who was probably a college student working at a summer job.

"I'd like the rooster," my father said. "How long has he been in the pot?" It was only good manners, as he knew it, to joke with people who waited on him.

"Beg your pardon?" the girl said.

"Roast chicken," said Beryl. "Is that okay for everybody?"

Mr. Florence was looking gloomy. Perhaps he didn't care for jokes when it was his money that was being spent. Perhaps he had counted on something better than ice water to fill up the glasses.

The waitress put down a dish of celery and olives, and my mother said, "Just a minute while I give thanks." She bowed her head and said quietly but audibly, "Lord, bless this food to our use, and us to Thy service, for Christ's sake. Amen." Refreshed, she sat up straight and passed the dish to me, saying, "Mind the olives. There's stones in them."

Beryl was smiling around at the room.

The waitress came back with a basket of rolls.

"Parker House!" Beryl leaned over and breathed in their smell. "Eat them while they're hot enough to melt the butter!"

Mr. Florence twitched, and peered into the butter dish. "Is that what this is—butter? I thought it was Shirley Temple's curls."

His face was hardly less gloomy than before, but it was a joke, and his making it seemed to convey to us something of the very thing that had just been publicly asked for—a blessing.

"When he says something funny," said Beryl—who often referred to Mr. Florence as "he" even when he was right there—"you notice how he always keeps a straight face? That reminds me of Mama. I mean of our mama, Marietta's and mine. Daddy, when he made a joke you could see it coming a mile away—he couldn't keep it off his face—but Mama was another story. She could look so sour. But she could joke on her deathbed. In fact, she did that very thing. Marietta, remember when she was in bed in the front room the spring before she died?"

"I remember she was in bed in that room," my mother said. "Yes."

"Well, Daddy came in and she was lying there in her clean nightgown, with the covers off, because the German lady from next door had just been helping her take a wash, and she was still there tidying up the bed. So Daddy wanted to be cheerful, and he said, 'Spring must be coming. I saw a crow today.' This must have been in March. And Mama said quick as a shot, 'Well, you better cover me up then, before it looks in that window and gets any ideas!' The German lady—Daddy said she just about dropped the basin. Because it was true, Mama was skin and bones; she was dying. But she could joke."

Mr. Florence said, "Might as well when there's no use to cry."

"But she could carry a joke too far, Mama could. One time,

one time, she wanted to give Daddy a scare. He was supposed to be interested in some girl that kept coming around to the works. Well, he was a big good-looking man. So Mama said, 'Well, I'll just do away with myself, and you can get on with her and see how you like it when I come back and haunt you.' He told her not to be so stupid, and he went off downtown. And Mama went out to the barn and climbed on a chair and put a rope around her neck. Didn't she, Marietta? Marietta went looking for her and she found her like that!"

My mother bent her head and put her hands in her lap, almost as if she was getting ready to say another grace.

"Daddy told me all about it, but I can remember anyway. I remember Marietta tearing off down the hill in her nightie, and I guess the German lady saw her go, and she came out and was looking for Mama, and somehow we all ended up in the barn—me, too, and some kids I was playing with—and there was Mama up on a chair preparing to give Daddy the fright of his life. She'd sent Marietta after him. And the German lady starts wailing, 'Oh, Missus, come down Missus, think of your little *kindren*'—'*kindren*' is the German for 'children'—'think of your *kindren*,' and so on. Until it was me standing there—I was just a little squirt, but I was the one noticed that rope. My eyes followed that rope up and up and I saw it was just hanging over the beam, just flung there—it wasn't tied at all! Marietta hadn't noticed that, the German lady hadn't noticed it. But I just spoke up and said, 'Mama, how are you going to manage to hang yourself without that rope tied around the beam?'"

Mr. Florence said, "That'd be a tough one."

"I spoiled her game. The German lady made coffee and we went over there and had a few treats, and, Marietta, you couldn't find Daddy after all, could you? You could hear Marietta howling, coming up the hill, a block away."

"Natural for her to be upset," my father said.

"Sure it was. Mama went too far."

"She meant it," my mother said. "She meant it more than you give her credit for."

"She meant to get a rise out of Daddy. That was their whole life together. He always said she was a hard woman to live with, but she had a lot of character. I believe he missed that, with Gladys."

"I wouldn't know," my mother said, in that particularly steady voice with which she always spoke of her father. "What he did say or didn't say."

"People are dead now," said my father. "It isn't up to us to judge."

"I know," said Beryl. "I know Marietta's always had a different view."

My mother looked at Mr. Florence and smiled quite easily and radiantly. "I'm sure you don't know what to make of all these family matters."

The one time that I visited Beryl, when Beryl was an old woman, all knobby and twisted up with arthritis, Beryl said, "Marietta got all Daddy's looks. And she never did a thing with herself. Remember her wearing that old navy-blue crêpe dress when we went to the hotel that time? Of course, I know it was probably all she had, but did it have to be all she had? You know, I was scared of her somehow. I couldn't stay in a room alone with her. But she had outstanding looks." Trying to remember an occasion when I had noticed my mother's looks, I thought of the time in the hotel, my mother's pale-olive skin against the heavy white, coiled hair, her open, handsome face smiling at Mr. Florence—as if he was the one to be forgiven.

———

I didn't have a problem right away with Beryl's story. For one thing, I was hungry and greedy, and a lot of my attention went to the roast chicken and gravy and mashed potatoes laid on the plate with an ice-cream scoop and the bright diced vegetables out of a can, which I thought much superior to those fresh from the garden. For dessert, I had a butterscotch sundae, an agonizing choice over chocolate. The others had plain vanilla ice cream.

Why shouldn't Beryl's version of the same event be different from my mother's? Beryl was strange in every way—everything about her was slanted, seen from a new angle. It was my mother's version that held, for a time. It absorbed Beryl's story, closed over it. But Beryl's story didn't vanish; it stayed sealed off for years, but it wasn't gone. It was like the knowledge of that hotel and dining room. I knew about it now, though I didn't think of it as a place to go back to. And indeed, without Beryl's or Mr. Florence's money, I couldn't. But I knew it was there.

The next time I was in the Wildwood Inn, in fact, was after I was married. The Lions Club had a banquet and dance there. The man I had married, Dan Casey, was a Lion. You could get a drink there by that time. Dan Casey wouldn't have gone anywhere you couldn't. Then the place was remodelled into the Hideaway, and now they have strippers every night but Sunday. On Thursday nights, they have a male stripper. I go there with people from the real-estate office to celebrate birthdays or other big events.

The farm was sold for five thousand dollars in 1965. A man from Toronto bought it, for a hobby farm or just an investment. After a couple of years, he rented it to a commune. They stayed there, different people drifting on and off, for a dozen years or so. They raised goats and sold the milk to the health-food store that had opened up in town. They painted a rainbow across the side of the barn that faced the road. They hung tie-dyed sheets over the windows, and let the long grass and flowering weeds reclaim the yard. My parents had finally got electricity in, but these people didn't use it. They preferred oil lamps and the wood stove, and taking their dirty clothes to town. People said they wouldn't know how to handle lamps or wood fires, and they would burn the place down. But they didn't. In fact, they didn't manage badly. They kept the house and barn in some sort of repair and they worked a big garden. They even dusted their potatoes against blight—though I heard that there was some sort of row about this and some of the stricter members left. The place actually looked a lot better than many of the farms round about that were still in the hands of the original families. The McAllister son had started a wrecking business on their place. My own brothers were long gone.

I knew I was not being reasonable, but I had the feeling that I'd rather see the farm suffer outright neglect—I'd sooner see it in the hands of hoodlums and scroungers—than see that rainbow on the barn, and some letters that looked Egyptian painted on the wall of the house. That seemed a mockery. I even disliked the sight of those people when they came to town—the men with their hair in ponytails, and with holes in their overalls that I believed were cut on purpose, and the women with long hair and no makeup and their meek, superior expressions. What do you know about life, I felt like asking them. What makes you think you can come here and mock my father and mother and their life and their poverty? But when I thought of the rainbow and those letters, I knew they weren't trying to mock or imitate my parents' life. They had displaced that life, hardly knowing it existed. They had set up in its place these beliefs and customs of their own, which I hoped would fail them.

That happened, more or less. The commune disintegrated. The goats disappeared. Some of the women moved to town, cut their hair, put on makeup, and got jobs as waitresses or cashiers to support their children. The Toronto man put the place up for sale, and after about a year it was sold for more than ten times what he had paid for it. A young couple from Ottawa bought it. They have painted the outside a pale gray with oyster trim, and have put in skylights and a handsome front door with carriage lamps on either side. Inside, they've changed it around so much that I've been told I'd never recognize it.

I did get in once, before this happened, during the year that the house was empty and for sale. The company I work for was handling it, and I had a key, though the house was being shown by another agent. I let myself in on a Sunday afternoon. I had a man with me, not a client but a friend—Bob Marks, whom I was seeing a lot at the time.

"This is that hippie place," Bob Marks said when I stopped the car. "I've been by here before."

He was a lawyer, a Catholic, separated from his wife. He thought he wanted to settle down and start up a practice here in town. But there already was one Catholic lawyer. Business was slow. A couple of times a week, Bob Marks would be fairly drunk before supper.

"It's more than that," I said. "It's where I was born. Where I grew up." We walked through the weeds, and I unlocked the door.

He said that he had thought, from the way I talked, that it would be farther out.

"It seemed farther then."

All the rooms were bare, and the floors swept clean. The

woodwork was freshly painted—I was surprised to see no smudges on the glass. Some new panes, some old wavy ones. Some of the walls had been stripped of their paper and painted. A wall in the kitchen was painted a deep blue, with an enormous dove on it. On a wall in the front room, giant sunflowers appeared, and a butterfly of almost the same size.

Bob Marks whistled. "Somebody was an artist."

"If that's what you want to call it," I said, and turned back to the kitchen. The same wood stove was there. "My mother once burned up three thousand dollars," I said. "She burned three thousand dollars in that stove."

He whistled again, differently. "What do you mean? She threw in a check?"

"No, no. It was bills. She did it deliberately. She went into town to the bank and she had them give it all to her, in a shoebox. She brought it home and put it in the stove. She put it in just a few bills at a time, so it wouldn't make too big a blaze. My father stood and watched her."

"What are you talking about?" said Bob Marks. "I thought you were so poor."

"We were. We were very poor."

"So how come she had three thousand dollars? That would be like thirty thousand today. Easily. More than thirty thousand today."

"It was her legacy," I said. "It was what she got from her father. Her father died in Seattle and left her three thousand dollars, and she burned it up because she hated him. She didn't want his money. She hated him."

"That's a lot of hate," Bob Marks said.

"That isn't the point. Her hating him, or whether he was bad enough for her to have a right to hate him. Not likely he was. That isn't the point."

"Money," he said. "Money's always the point."

"No. My father letting her do it is the point. To me it is. My father stood and watched and he never protested. If anybody had tried to stop her, he would have protected her. I consider that love."

"Some people would consider it lunacy."

I remember that that had been Beryl's opinion, exactly.

I went into the front room and stared at the butterfly, with its pink-and-orange wings. Then I went into the front bedroom and found two human figures painted on the wall. A man and a woman holding hands and facing straight ahead. They were naked, and larger than life size.

"It reminds me of that John Lennon and Yoko Ono picture," I said to Bob Marks, who had come in behind me. "That record cover, wasn't it?" I didn't want him to think that anything he had said in the kitchen had upset me.

Bob Marks said, "Different color hair."

That was true. Both figures had yellow hair painted in a solid mass, the way they do it in the comic strips. Horsetails of yellow hair curling over their shoulders and little pigs' tails of yellow hair decorating their not so private parts. Their skin was a flat beige pink and their eyes a staring blue, the same blue that was on the kitchen wall.

I noticed that they hadn't quite finished peeling the wallpaper away before making this painting. In the corner, there was some paper left that matched the paper on the other walls—a modernistic design of intersecting pink and gray and mauve bubbles. The man from Toronto must have put that on. The paper underneath hadn't been stripped off when this new paper went on. I could see an edge of it, the cornflowers on a white ground.

"I guess this was where they carried on their sexual shenanigans," Bob Marks said, in a tone familiar to me. That thickened, sad, uneasy, but determined tone. The not particularly friendly lust of middle-aged respectable men.

I didn't say anything. I worked away some of the bubble paper to see more of the cornflowers. Suddenly I hit a loose spot, and ripped away a big swatch of it. But the cornflower paper came, too, and a little shower of dried plaster.

"Why is it?" I said. "Just tell me, why is it that no man can mention a place like this without getting around to the subject of sex in about two seconds flat? Just say the words 'hippie' or 'commune' and all you guys can think about is screwing! As if there wasn't anything at all behind it but orgies and fancy combinations and non-stop screwing! I get so sick of that—it's all so stupid it just makes me sick!"

In the car on the way home from the hotel, we sat as before—the men in the front seat, the women in the back. I was in the middle, Beryl and my mother on either side of me. Their heated bodies pressed against me, through cloth; their smells crowded out the smells of the cedar bush we passed through, and the pockets of bog, where Beryl exclaimed at the water lilies. Beryl smelled of all those things in pots and bottles. My mother smelled of flour and hard soap and the warm crêpe of her good dress and the kerosene she had used to take the spots off.

"A lovely meal," my mother said. "Thank you, Beryl. Thank you, Mr. Florence."

"I don't know who is going to be fit to do the milking," my father said. "Now that we've all ate in such style."

"Speaking of money," said Beryl—though nobody actually had been—"do you mind my asking what you did with yours? I put mine in real estate. Real estate in California—you can't lose. I was thinking you could get an electric stove, so you wouldn't have to bother with a fire in summer or fool with that coal-oil thing, either one."

All the other people in the car laughed, even Mr. Florence.

"That's a good idea, Beryl," said my father. "We could use it to set things on till we get the electricity."

"Oh, Lord," said Beryl. "How stupid can I get?"

"And we don't actually have the money, either," my mother said cheerfully, as if she was continuing the joke.

But Beryl spoke sharply. "You wrote me you got it. You got the same as me."

My father half turned in his seat. "What money are you talking about?" he said. "What's this money?"

"From Daddy's will," Beryl said. "That you got last year. Look, maybe I shouldn't have asked. If you had to pay something off, that's still a good use, isn't it? It doesn't matter. We're all family here. Practically."

"We didn't have to use it to pay anything off," my mother said. "I burned it."

Then she told how she went into town in the truck, one day almost a year ago, and got them to give her the money in a box she had brought along for the purpose. She took it home, and put it in the stove and burned it.

My father turned around and faced the road ahead.

I could feel Beryl twisting beside me while my mother talked. She was twisting, and moaning a little, as if she had a pain she couldn't suppress. At the end of the story, she let out a sound of astonishment and suffering, an angry groan.

"So you burned up money!" she said. "You burned up money in the stove."

My mother was still cheerful. "You sound as if I'd burned up one of my children."

"You burned their chances. You burned up everything the money could have got for them."

"The last thing my children need is money. None of us need his money."

"That's criminal," Beryl said harshly. She pitched her voice into the front seat: "Why did you let her?"

"He wasn't there," my mother said. "Nobody was there."

My father said, "It was her money, Beryl."

"Never mind," Beryl said. "That's criminal."

"Criminal is for when you call in the police," Mr. Florence said. Like other things he had said that day, this created a little island of surprise and a peculiar gratitude.

Gratitude not felt by all.

"Don't you pretend this isn't the craziest thing you ever heard of," Beryl shouted into the front seat. "Don't you pretend you don't think so! Because it is, and you do. You think just the same as me!"

My father did not stand in the kitchen watching my mother feed the money into the flames. It wouldn't appear so. He did not know about it—it seems fairly clear, if I remember everything, that he did not know about it until that Sunday afternoon in Mr. Florence's Chrysler, when my mother told them all together. Why, then, can I see the scene so clearly, just as I described it to Bob Marks (and to others—he was not the first)? I see my father standing by the table in the middle of the room—the table with the drawer in it for knives and forks, and the scrubbed oilcloth on top—and there is the box of money on the table. My mother is carefully dropping the bills into the fire. She holds the stove lid by the blackened lifter in one hand. And my father, standing by, seems not just to be permitting her to do this but to be protecting her. A solemn scene, but not crazy. People doing something that seems to them natural and necessary. At least, one of them is doing what seems natural and necessary, and the other believes that the important thing is for that person to be free, to go ahead. They understand that other people might not think so. They do not care.

How hard it is for me to believe that I made that up. It seems so much the truth it is the truth; it's what I believe about them. I haven't stopped believing it. But I have stopped telling that story. I never told it to anyone again after telling it to Bob Marks. I don't think so. I didn't stop just because it wasn't, strictly speaking, true. I stopped because I saw that I had to give up expecting people to see it the way I did. I had to give up expecting them to approve of any part of what was done. How could I even say that I approved of it myself? If I had been the sort of person who approved of that, who could do it, I wouldn't have done all I have done—run away from home to work in a restaurant in town when I was fifteen, gone to night school to learn typing and bookkeeping, got into the real-estate office, and finally become a licensed agent. I wouldn't be divorced. My father wouldn't have died in the county home. My hair would be white, as it has been naturally for years, instead of a color called Copper Sunrise. And not one of these things would I change, not really, if I could.

Bob Marks was a decent man—good-hearted, sometimes with imagination. After I had lashed out at him like that, he said, "You don't need to be so tough on us." In a moment, he said, "Was this your room when you were a little girl?" He thought that was why the mention of the sexual shenanigans had upset me.

And I thought it would be just as well to let him think that. I said yes, yes, it was my room when I was a little girl. It was just as well to make up right away. Moments of kindness and reconciliation are worth having, even if the parting has to come sooner or later. I wonder if those moments aren't more valued, and deliberately gone after, in the setups some people like myself have now, than they were in those old marriages, where love and grudges could be growing underground, so confused and stubborn, it must have seemed they had forever.

DIFFERENTLY

Georgia once took a creative-writing course, and what the instructor told her was: Too many things. Too many things going on at the same time; also too many people. Think, he told her. What is the important thing? What do you want us to pay attention to? Think.

Eventually she wrote a story that was about her grandfather killing chickens, and the instructor seemed to be pleased with it. Georgia herself thought that it was a fake. She made a long list of all the things that had been left out and handed it in as an appendix to the story. The instructor said that she expected too much, of herself and of the process, and that she was wearing him out.

The course was not a total loss, because Georgia and the instructor ended up living together. They still live together, in Ontario, on a farm. They sell raspberries, and run a small publishing business. When Georgia can get the money together, she goes to Vancouver to visit her sons. This fall Saturday she has taken the ferry across to Victoria, where she used to live. She did this on an impulse that she doesn't really trust, and by midafternoon, when she walks up the driveway of the splendid stone house where she used to visit Maya, she has already been taken over some fairly shaky ground.

When she phoned Raymond, she wasn't sure that he would ask her to the house. She wasn't sure that she even wanted to go there. She had no notion of how welcome she would be. But Raymond opens the door before she can touch the bell, and he hugs her around the shoulders and kisses her twice (surely he didn't use to do this?) and introduces his wife, Anne. He says he has told her what great friends they were, Georgia and Ben and he and Maya. Great friends.

Maya is dead. Georgia and Ben are long divorced.

They go and sit in what Maya used to call, with a certain flat cheerfulness, "the family room."

(One evening Raymond had said to Ben and Georgia that it looked as if Maya wasn't going to be able to have any children. "We try our best," he said. "We use pillows and everything. But no luck."

"Listen, old man, you don't do it with pillows," Ben said boisterously. They were all a little drunk. "I thought you were the expert on all the apparatus, but I can see that you and I are going to have to have a little talk."

Raymond was an obstetrician and gynecologist.

By that time Georgia knew all about the abortion in Seattle, which had been set up by Maya's lover, Harvey. Harvey was also a doctor, a surgeon. The bleak apartment in the run-down building, the bad-tempered old woman who was knitting a sweater, the doctor arriving in his shirtsleeves, carrying a brown-paper bag that Maya hysterically believed must contain the tools of his trade. In fact, it contained his lunch—an egg-and-onion sandwich. Maya had the smell of that in her face all the time he and Mme. Defarge were working her over.

Maya and Georgia smiled at each other primly while their husbands continued their playful conversation.)

Raymond's curly brown hair has turned into a silvery fluff, and his face is lined. But nothing dreadful has happened to him—no pouches or jowls or alcoholic flush or sardonic droop of defeat. He is still thin, and straight, and sharp-shouldered, still fresh-smelling, spotless, appropriately, expensively dressed. He'll make a brittle, elegant old man, with an obliging boy's smile. There's that sort of shine on both of them, Maya once said glumly. She was speaking of Raymond and Ben. Maybe we should soak them in vinegar, she said.

The room has changed more than Raymond has. An ivory leather sofa has replaced Maya's tapestry-covered couch, and of course all the old opium-den clutter, Maya's cushions and pampas grass and the gorgeous multicolored elephant with the tiny sewn-on mirrors—that's all gone. The room is beige and ivory, smooth and comfortable as the new blond wife, who sits on the arm of Raymond's chair and maneuvers his arm around her, placing his hand on her thigh. She wears slick-looking white pants and a cream-on-white appliquéd sweater, with gold jewelry. Raymond gives her a couple of hearty and defiant pats.

"Are you going someplace?" he says. "Possibly shopping?"

"Righto," says the wife. "Old times." She smiles at Georgia. "It's okay," she says. "I really do have to go shopping."

When she has gone, Raymond pours drinks for Georgia and himself. "Anne is a worrywart about the booze," he says. "She won't put salt on the table. She threw out all the curtains in the house to get rid of the smell of Maya's cigarettes. I know what you may be thinking: Friend Raymond has got hold of a luscious blonde. But this is actually a very serious girl, and a very steady girl. I had her in my office, you know, quite a while before Maya died. I mean, I had her *working* in my office. I don't mean that the way it sounds! She isn't as young as she looks, either. She's thirty-six."

Georgia had thought forty. She is tired of the visit already, but she has to tell about herself. No, she is not married. Yes, she works. She and the friend she lives with have a farm and a publishing business. Touch and go, not much money. Interesting. A male friend, yes.

"I've lost all track of Ben somehow," Raymond says. "The last I heard, he was living on a boat."

"He and his wife sail around the West Coast every summer," Georgia says. "In the winter they go to Hawaii. The Navy lets you retire early."

"Marvellous," says Raymond.

Seeing Raymond has made Georgia think that she has no idea what Ben looks like now. Has he gone white-haired, has he thickened around the middle? Both of these things have happened to her—she has turned into a chunky woman with a healthy olive skin, a crest of white hair, wearing loose and rather splashy clothes. When she thinks of Ben, she sees him still as a handsome Navy officer, with a perfect Navy look—keen and serious and self-effacing. The look of someone who longed, bravely, to be given orders. Her sons must have pictures of him around—they both see him, they spend holidays on his boat. Perhaps they put the pictures away when she comes to visit. Perhaps they think of protecting these images of him from one who did him hurt.

On the way to Maya's house—Raymond's house—Georgia walked past another house, which she could easily have avoided. A house in Oak Bay, which in fact she had to go out of her way to see.

It was still the house that she and Ben had read about in the real-estate columns of the Victoria *Colonist*. Roomy bungalow under picturesque oak trees. Arbutus, dogwood, window seats, fireplace, diamond-paned windows, character. Georgia stood outside the gate and felt a most predictable pain. Here Ben had cut the grass, here the children had made their paths and hideaways in the bushes, and laid out a graveyard for the birds and snakes killed by the black cat, Domino. She could recall the

inside of the house perfectly—the oak floors she and Ben had
laboriously sanded, the walls they had painted, the room
where she had lain in drugged misery after having her wisdom
teeth out. Ben had read aloud to her, from *Dubliners.* She
couldn't remember the title of the story. It was about a timid
poetic sort of young man, with a mean pretty wife. Poor bug-
ger, said Ben when he'd finished it.

Ben liked fiction, which was surprising in a man who also
liked sports, and had been popular at school.

She ought to have stayed away from this neighborhood.
Everywhere she walked here, under the chestnut trees with
their flat gold leaves, and the red-limbed arbutus, and the tall
Garry oaks, which suggested fairy stories, European forests,
woodcutters, witches—everywhere her footsteps reproached
her, saying *what-for, what-for, what-for.* This reproach was just
what she had expected—it was what she courted—and there
was something cheap about doing such a thing. Something
cheap and useless. She knew it. But *what-for, what-for, what-for,
wrong-and-waste, wrong-and-waste* went her silly, censorious feet.

Raymond wants Georgia to look at the garden, which he
says was made for Maya during the last months of her life.
Maya designed it; then she lay on the tapestry couch (setting
fire to it twice, Raymond says, by dozing off with a cigarette
lit), and she was able to see it all take shape.

Georgia sees a pond, a stone-rimmed pond with an island
in the middle. The head of a wicked-looking stone beast—
a mountain goat?—rears up on the island, spouting water.
Around the pond a jungle of Shasta daisies, pink and purple
cosmos, dwarf pines and cypresses, some other miniature tree
with glossy red leaves. On the island, now that she looks more
closely, are mossy stone walls—the ruins of a tiny tower.

"She hired a young chap to do the work," Raymond says.
"She lay there and watched him. It took all summer. She just

lay all day and watched him making her garden. Then he'd
come in and they'd have tea, and talk about it. You know, Maya
didn't just design that garden. She imagined it. She'd tell him
what she'd been imagining about it, and he'd take off from
there. I mean, this to them was not just a garden. The pond was
a lake in this country they had some name for, and all around
the lake were forests and territories where different tribes and
factions lived. Do you get the picture?"

"Yes," says Georgia.

"Maya had a dazzling imagination. She could have written
fantasy or science fiction. Whatever. She was a creative person,
without any doubt about it. But you could not get her to seriously use her creativity. That goat was one of the gods of that
country, and the island was like a sacred place with a former
temple on it. You can see the ruins. They had the religion all
worked out. Oh, and the literature, the poems and the legends
and the history—everything. They had a song that the queen
would sing. Of course it was supposed to be a translation, from
that language. They had some of that figured out too. There had
been a queen that was shut up in that ruin. That temple. I forget why. She was getting sacrificed, probably. Getting her heart
torn out or some gruesome thing. It was all complicated and
melodramatic. But think of the effort that went into it. The
creativity. The young chap was an artist by profession. I believe
he thought of himself as an artist. I don't know how she got
hold of him, actually. She knew people. He supported himself
doing this kind of thing, I imagine. He did a good job. He laid
the pipes, everything. He showed up every day. Every day he
came in when he was finished and had tea and talked to her.
Well, in my opinion, they didn't just have tea. To my knowledge, not just tea. He would bring a little substance, they would
have a little smoke. I told Maya she should write it all down.

"But you know, the instant he was finished, off he went. Off he went. I don't know. Maybe he got another job. It didn't seem to me that it was my place to ask. But I did think that even if he had got a job he could have come back and visited her now and then. Or if he'd gone off on a trip somewhere he could have written letters. I thought he could have. I expected that much of him. It wouldn't have been any skin off his back. Not as I see it. It would have been nice of him to make her think that it hadn't been just a case of—of hired friendship, you know, all along."

Raymond is smiling. He cannot repress, or perhaps is not aware of, this smile.

"For that was the conclusion she must have come to," he says. "After all that nice time and imagining together· and egging each other on. She must have been disappointed. She must have been. Even at that stage, such a thing would matter a lot to her. You and I know it, Georgia. It would have mattered. He could have treated her a little more kindly. It wouldn't have had to be for very long."

Maya died a year ago, in the fall, but Georgia did not hear about it until Christmas. She got the news in Hilda's Christmas letter. Hilda, who used to be married to Harvey, is now married to another doctor, in a town in the interior of British Columbia. A few years ago she and Georgia, both visitors, met by chance on a Vancouver street, and they have written occasional letters since.

Of course you knew Maya so much better than I did, Hilda wrote. *But I've been surprised how often I've thought about her. I've been thinking of all of us, really, how we were, fifteen or so years ago, and I think we were just as vulnerable in some ways as the kids with their acid trips and so on, that were supposed to be marked for life. Weren't we marked—all of us smashing up our marriages and going out look-*

ing for adventure? Of course, Maya didn't smash up her marriage, she
of all people stayed where she was, so I suppose it doesn't make much
sense what I'm saying. But Maya seemed the most vulnerable person of
all to me, so gifted and brittle. I remember I could hardly bear to look at
that vein in her temple where she parted her hair.

What an odd letter for Hilda to write, thought Georgia. She
remembered Hilda's expensive pastel plaid shirtdresses, her
neat, short, fair hair, her good manners. Did Hilda really think
she had smashed up her marriage and gone out looking for
adventure under the influence of dope and rock music and
revolutionary costumes? Georgia's impression was that Hilda
had left Harvey, once she found out what he was up to—or
some of what he was up to—and gone to the town in the interior where she sensibly took up her old profession of nursing
and in due time married another, presumably more trustwor-
thy doctor. Maya and Georgia had never thought of Hilda as a
woman like themselves. And Hilda and Maya had not been
close—they had particular reason not to be. But Hilda had kept
track; she knew of Maya's death, she wrote these generous
words. Without Hilda, Georgia would not have known. She
would still have been thinking that someday she might write to
Maya, there might come a time when their friendship could
be mended.

The first time that Ben and Georgia went to Maya's house,
Harvey and Hilda were there. Maya was having a dinner party
for just the six of them. Georgia and Ben had recently moved
to Victoria, and Ben had phoned Raymond, who had been a
friend of his at school. Ben had never met Maya, but he told
Georgia that he had heard that she was very clever, and weird.
People said that she was weird. But she was rich—an heiress—
so she could get away with it.

Georgia groaned at the news that Maya was rich, and she groaned again at the sight of the house—the great stone-block house with its terraced lawns and clipped bushes and circular drive.

Georgia and Ben came from the same small town in Ontario, and had the same sort of families. It was a fluke that Ben had been sent to a good private school—the money had come from a great-aunt. Even in her teens, when she was proud of being Ben's girl and prouder than she liked to let on about being asked to the dances at that school, Georgia had a low opinion of the girls she met there. She thought rich girls were spoiled and brainless. She called them twits. She thought of herself as a girl—and then a woman—who didn't much like other girls and women. She called the other Navy wives "the Navy *ladies.*" Ben was sometimes entertained by her opinions of people and at other times asked if it was really necessary to be so critical.

He had an inkling, he said, that she was going to like Maya. This didn't predispose Georgia in Maya's favor. But Ben turned out to be right. He was very happy then, to have come up with somebody like Maya as an offering to Georgia, to have found a couple with whom he and Georgia could willingly link up as friends. "It'll be good for us to have some non-Navy friends," he was to say. "Some wife for you to knock around with who isn't so conventional. You can't say Maya's conventional."

Georgia couldn't. The house was more or less what she had expected—soon she learned that Maya called it "your friendly neighborhood fortress"—but Maya was a surprise. She opened the door herself, barefoot, wearing a long shapeless robe of coarse brown cloth that looked like burlap. Her hair was long and straight, parted high at one temple. It was almost the same dull-brown color as the robe. She did not wear lipstick, and her skin was rough and pale, with marks like faint bird tracks in the hollows of her cheeks. This lack of color, this roughness of texture about her seemed a splendid assertion of quality. How indifferent she looked, how arrogant and indifferent, with her bare feet, her unpainted toenails, her queer robe. The only thing that she had done to her face was to paint her eyebrows blue—to pluck out all the hairs of her eyebrows, in fact, and paint the skin blue. Not an arched line—just a little daub of blue over each eye, like a swollen vein.

Georgia, whose dark hair was teased, whose eyes were painted in the style of the time, whose breasts were stylishly proffered, found all this disconcerting, and wonderful.

Harvey was the other person there whose looks Georgia found impressive. He was a short man with heavy shoulders, a slight potbelly, puffy blue eyes, and a pugnacious expression. He came from Lancashire. His gray hair was thin on top but worn long at the sides—combed over his ears in a way that made him look more like an artist than a surgeon. "He doesn't even look to me exactly clean enough to be a surgeon," Georgia said to Ben afterward. "Wouldn't you think he'd be something like a sculptor? With gritty fingernails? I expect he treats women badly." She was recalling how he had looked at her breasts. "Not like Raymond," she said. "Raymond worships Maya. And he is extremely clean."

(Raymond has the kind of looks everybody's mother is crazy about, Maya was to say to Georgia, with slashing accuracy, a few weeks after this.)

The food that Maya served was no better than you would expect at a family dinner, and the heavy silver forks were slightly tarnished. But Raymond poured good wine that he would have liked to talk about. He did not manage to interrupt Harvey, who told scandalous and indiscreet hospital stories, and was blandly outrageous about necrophilia and masturbation. Later, in the living room, the coffee was made and served with some ceremony. Raymond got everybody's attention as he ground the beans in a Turkish cylinder. He talked about the importance of the aromatic oils. Harvey, halted in mid-anecdote, watched with an unkindly smirk, Hilda with patient polite attention. It was Maya who gave her husband radiant encouragement, hung about him like an acolyte, meekly and gracefully assisting. She served the coffee in beautiful little Turkish cups, which she and Raymond had bought in a shop in San Francisco, along with the coffee grinder. She listened demurely to Raymond talking about the shop, as if she recalled other holiday pleasures.

Harvey and Hilda were the first to leave. Maya hung on Raymond's shoulder, saying good-bye. But she detached herself once they were gone, her slithery grace and wifely demeanor discarded. She stretched out casually and awkwardly on the sofa and said, "Now, don't you go yet. Nobody gets half a chance to talk while Harvey is around—you have to talk after."

And Georgia saw how it was. She saw that Maya was hoping not to be left alone with the husband whom she had aroused—for whatever purposes—by her showy attentions. She saw that Maya was mournful and filled with a familiar dread at the end of her dinner party. Raymond was happy. He sat down on the end of the sofa, lifting Maya's reluctant feet to do so. He rubbed one of her feet between his hands.

"What a savage," Raymond said. "This is a woman who won't wear shoes."

"Brandy!" said Maya, springing up. "I knew there was something else you did at dinner parties. You drink brandy!"

"He loves her but she doesn't love him," said Georgia to Ben, just after she had remarked on Raymond's worshipping Maya and being very clean. But Ben, perhaps not listening carefully, thought she was talking about Harvey and Hilda.

"No, no, no. There I think it's the other way round. It's hard to tell with English people. Maya was putting on an act for them. I have an idea about why."

"You have an idea about everything," said Ben.

Georgia and Maya became friends on two levels. On the first level, they were friends as wives; on the second as themselves. On the first level, they had dinner at each other's houses. They listened to their husbands talk about their school days. The jokes and fights, the conspiracies and disasters, the bullies and the victims. Terrifying or pitiable schoolfellows and teachers, treats and humiliations. Maya asked if they were sure they hadn't read all that in a book. "It sounds just like a story," she said. "A boys' story about school."

They said that their experiences were what the books were all about. When they had talked enough about school, they talked about movies, politics, public personalities, places they had travelled to or wanted to travel to. Maya and Georgia could join in then. Ben and Raymond did not believe in leaving women out of the conversation. They believed that women were every bit as intelligent as men.

On the second level, Georgia and Maya talked in each other's kitchens, over coffee. Or they had lunch downtown. There were two places, and only two, where Maya liked to have lunch. One was the Moghul's Court—a seedy, grandiose bar in a large, grim railway hotel. The Moghul's Court had curtains of moth-eaten pumpkin-colored velvet, and desiccated ferns, and waiters who wore turbans. Maya always dressed up to go there, in droopy, silky dresses and not very clean white gloves and amazing hats that she found in secondhand stores. She pretended to be a widow who had served with her husband in various outposts of the Empire. She spoke in fluty tones to the sullen young waiters, asking them, "Could you be so good as to . . ." and then telling them they had been terribly, terribly kind.

She and Georgia worked out the history of the Empire widow, and Georgia was added to the story as a grumpy, secretly Socialistic hired companion named Miss Amy Jukes. The widow's name was Mrs. Allegra Forbes-Bellyea. Her husband had been Nigel Forbes-Bellyea. Sometimes Sir Nigel. Most of one rainy afternoon in the Moghul's Court was spent in devising the horrors of the Forbes-Bellyea honeymoon, in a damp hotel in Wales.

The other place that Maya liked was a hippie restaurant on Blanshard Street, where you sat on dirty plush cushions tied to the tops of stumps and ate brown rice with slimy vegetables and drank cloudy cider. (At the Moghul's Court, Maya and Georgia drank only gin.) When they lunched at the hippie restaurant, they wore long, cheap, pretty Indian cotton dresses and pretended to be refugees from a commune, where they had both been the attendants or concubines of a folksinger named Bill Bones. They made up several songs for Bill Bones, all mild and tender blue-eyed songs that contrasted appallingly with his greedy and licentious ways. Bill Bones had very curious personal habits.

When they weren't playing these games, they talked in a headlong fashion about their lives, childhoods, problems, husbands.

"That was a horrible place," Maya said. "That school."

Georgia agreed.

"They were poor boys at a rich kids' school," Maya said. "So they had to try hard. They had to be a credit to their families."

Georgia would not have thought Ben's family poor, but she knew that there were different ways of looking at such things.

Maya said that whenever they had people in for dinner or the evening, Raymond would pick out beforehand all the records he thought suitable and put them in a suitable order. "I think sometime he'll hand out conversational topics at the door," Maya said.

Georgia revealed that Ben wrote a letter every week to the great-aunt who had sent him to school.

"Is it a nice letter?" said Maya.

"Yes. Oh, yes. It's very nice."

They looked at each other bleakly, and laughed. Then they announced—they admitted—what weighed on them. It was the innocence of these husbands—the hearty, decent, firm, contented innocence. That is a wearying and finally discouraging thing. It makes intimacy a chore.

"But do you feel badly," Georgia said, "talking like this?"

"Of course," said Maya, grinning and showing her large perfect teeth—the product of expensive dental work from the days before she had charge of her own looks. "I have another reason to feel badly," she said. "But I don't know whether I do. I do and I don't."

"I know," said Georgia, who up until that moment hadn't known, for sure.

"You're very smart," Maya said. "Or I'm very obvious. What do you think of him?"

"A lot of trouble," Georgia said judiciously. She was pleased with that answer, which didn't show how flattered she felt by the disclosure, or how heady she found this conversation.

"You aren't just a-whistlin' 'Dixie,'" Maya said, and she told the story about the abortion. "I am going to break up with him," she said. "Any day now."

But she kept on seeing Harvey. She would relate, at lunch, some very disillusioning facts about him, then announce that she had to go, she was meeting him at a motel out on the Gorge Road, or at the cabin he had on Prospect Lake.

"Must scrub," she said.

She had left Raymond once. Not for Harvey. She had run away with, or to, a musician. A pianist—Nordic and sleepy-looking but bad-tempered—from her society-lady, symphony-benefit days. She travelled with him for five weeks, and he deserted her in a hotel in Cincinnati. She then developed frightful chest pains, appropriate to a breaking heart. What she really had was a gallbladder attack. Raymond was sent for, and he came and got her out of the hospital. They had a little holiday in Mexico before they came home.

"That was it, for me," Maya said. "That was your true and desperate love. Nevermore."

What then, was Harvey?

"Exercise," said Maya.

Georgia got a part-time job in a bookstore, working several evenings a week. Ben went away on his yearly cruise. The summer turned out to be unusually hot and sunny for the West Coast. Georgia combed her hair out and stopped using most of her makeup and bought a couple of short halter dresses. Sitting on her stool at the front of the store, showing her bare brown shoulders and sturdy brown legs, she looked like a college girl—clever but full of energy and bold opinions. The people who came into the store liked the look of a girl—a woman—like Georgia. They liked to talk to her. Most of them came in alone. They were not exactly lonely people, but they were lonely for somebody to talk to about books. Georgia plugged in the kettle behind the desk and made mugs of raspberry tea. Some favored customers brought in their own mugs. Maya came to visit and lurked about in the background, amused and envious.

"You know what you've got?" she said to Georgia. "You've got a salon! Oh, I'd like to have a job like that! I'd even like an ordinary job in an ordinary store, where you fold things up and find things for people and make change and say thank you very much, and colder out today, will it rain?"

"You could get a job like that," said Georgia.

"No, I couldn't. I don't have the discipline. I was too badly brought up. I can't even keep house without Mrs. Hanna and Mrs. Cheng and Sadie."

It was true. Maya had a lot of servants, for a modern woman, though they came at different times and did separate things and were nothing like an old-fashioned household staff. Even the food at her dinner parties, which seemed to show her own indifferent touch, had been prepared by someone else.

Usually, Maya was busy in the evenings. Georgia was just as glad, because she didn't really want Maya coming into the store, asking for crazy titles that she had made up, making Georgia's employment there a kind of joke. Georgia took the store seriously. She had a serious, secret liking for it that she could not explain. It was a long, narrow store with an old-fashioned funnelled entryway between two angled display windows. From her stool behind the desk Georgia was able to see the reflections in one window reflected in the other. This street was not one of those decked out to receive tourists. It was a wide east-west street filled in the early evening with a faintly yellow light, a light reflected off pale stucco buildings that were not very high, plain storefronts, nearly empty sidewalks. Georgia found this plainness liberating after the winding shady streets, the flowery yards and vine-framed windows of Oak Bay. Here the books could come into their own, as they never could in a more artful and enticing suburban bookshop. Straight long rows of paperbacks. (Most of the Penguins then still had their orange-and-white or blue-and-white covers, with no designs or pictures, just the unadorned, unexplained titles.) The store was a straight avenue of bounty, of plausible promises. Certain books that Georgia had never read, and probably never would read, were important to her, because of the stateliness or mystery of their titles. *In Praise of Folly. The Roots of Coincidence. The Flowering of New England. Ideas and Integrities.* Sometimes she got up and put the books in stricter order. The fiction was shelved alphabetically, by author, which was sensible but not very interesting. The history books, however, and the philosophy and psychology and other science books were arranged according to certain intricate and delightful rules—having to do with chronology and content—that Georgia grasped immediately and even elaborated on. She did not need to read much of a book to know about it. She got a sense of it easily, almost at once, as if by smell.

At times the store was empty, and she felt an abundant calm. It was not even the books that mattered then. She sat on the stool and watched the street—patient, expectant, by herself, in a finely balanced and suspended state.

She saw Miles' reflection—his helmeted ghost parking his motorcycle at the curb—before she saw him. She believed that she had noted his valiant profile, his pallor, his dusty red hair (he took off his helmet and shook out his hair before coming into the store), and his quick, slouching, insolent, invading way of moving, even in the glass.

It was no surprise that he soon began to talk to her, as others did. He told her that he was a diver. He looked for wrecks, and lost airplanes, and dead bodies. He had been hired by a rich couple in Victoria who were planning a treasure-hunting cruise, getting it together at the moment. Their names, the destination were all secrets. Treasure-hunting was a lunatic business. He had done it before. His home was in Seattle, where he had a wife and a little daughter.

Everything he told her could easily have been a lie.

He showed her pictures in books—photographs and drawings, of mollusks, jellyfish, the Portuguese man-of-war, sargasso weed, the Caribbean flying fish, the girdle of Venus. He pointed out which pictures were accurate, which were fakes. Then he went away and paid no more attention to her, even slipping out of the store while she was busy with a customer. Not a hint of a good-bye. But he came in another evening, and told her about a drowned man wedged into the cabin of a boat, looking out the watery window in an interested way. By attention and avoidance, impersonal conversations in close proximity, by his oblivious prowling, and unsmiling, lengthy, gray-eyed looks, he soon had Georgia in a disturbed and not disagreeable state. He stayed away two nights in a row, then came in and asked her, abruptly, if she would like a ride home on his motorcycle.

Georgia said yes. She had never ridden on a motorcycle in her life. Her car was in the parking lot; she knew what was bound to happen.

She told him where she lived. "Just a few blocks up from the beach," she said.

"We'll go to the beach, then. We'll go and sit on the logs."

That was what they did. They sat for a while on the logs. Then, though the beach was not quite dark or completely deserted, they made love in the imperfect shelter of some broom bushes. Georgia walked home, a strengthened and lightened woman, not in the least in love, favored by the universe.

"My car wouldn't start," she told the baby-sitter, a grandmother from down the street. "I walked all the way home. It was lovely, walking. Lovely. I enjoyed it so much."

Her hair was wild, her lips were swollen, her clothes were full of sand.

Her life filled up with such lies. Her car would be parked beside outlying beaches, on the logging roads so conveniently close to the city, on the wandering back roads of the Saanich Peninsula. The map of the city that she had held in her mind up till now, with its routes to shops and work and friends' houses, was overlaid with another map, of circuitous routes followed in fear (not shame) and excitement, of flimsy shelters, temporary hiding places, where she and Miles made love, often within hearing distance of passing traffic or a hiking party or a family picnic. And Georgia herself, watching her children on the roundabout, or feeling the excellent shape of a lemon in her hand at the supermarket, contained another woman, who only a few hours before had been whimpering and tussling on the ferns, on the sand, on the bare ground, or, during a rainstorm, in her own car—who had been driven hard and gloriously out of her mind and drifted loose and gathered her wits and made her way home again. Was this a common story? Georgia cast an eye over the other women at the supermarket. She looked for signs—of dreaminess or flaunting, a sense of drama in a woman's way of dressing, a special rhythm in her movements.

How many, she asked Maya.

"God knows," said Maya. "Do a survey."

Trouble began, perhaps, as soon as they said that they loved each other. Why did they do that—defining, inflating, obscuring whatever it was they did feel? It seemed to be demanded, that was all—just the way changes, variations, elaborations in the lovemaking itself might be demanded. It was a way of going further. So they said it, and that night Georgia couldn't sleep. She did not regret what had been said or think that it was a lie, though she knew that it was absurd. She thought of the way Miles sought to have her look into his eyes during lovemaking—something Ben expressly did not do—and she thought of how his eyes, at first bright and challenging, became cloudy and calm and somber. That way she trusted him—it was the only way. She thought of being launched out on a gray, deep, baleful, magnificent sea. Love.

"I didn't know this was going to happen," she said in Maya's kitchen the next day, drinking her coffee. The day was warm, but she had put on a sweater to huddle in. She felt shaken, and submissive.

"No. And you don't know," said Maya rather sharply. "Did he say it too? Did he say he loved you too?"

Yes, said Georgia, yes, of course.

"Look out, then. Look out for next time. Next time is always pretty tricky when they've said that."

And so it was. Next time a rift opened. At first they simply tested it, to see if it was there. It was almost like a new diversion to them. But it widened, it widened. Before any words were said to confirm that it was there, Georgia felt it widen, she coldly felt it widen, though she was desperate for it to close. Did he feel the same thing? She didn't know. He too seemed cold—pale, deliberate, glittering with some new malicious intent.

They were sitting recklessly, late at night, in Georgia's car among the other lovers at Clover Point.

"Everybody here in these cars doing the same thing we're doing," Miles had said. "Doesn't that idea turn you on?"

He had said that at the very moment in their ritual when they had been moved, last time, to speak brokenly and solemnly of love.

"You ever think of that?" he said. "I mean, we could start with Ben and Laura. You ever imagine how it would be with you and me and Ben and Laura?"

Laura was his wife, at home in Seattle. He had not spoken of her before, except to tell Georgia her name. He had spoken of Ben, in a way that Georgia didn't like but passed over.

"What does Ben think you do for fun," he'd said, "while he is off cruising the ocean blue?"

"Do you and Ben usually have a big time when he gets back?"

"Does Ben like that outfit as much as I do?"

He spoke as if he and Ben were friends in some way, or at least partners, co-proprietors.

"You and me and Ben and Laura," he said, in a tone that seemed to Georgia insistently and artificially lecherous, sly, derisive. "Spread the joy around."

He tried to fondle her, pretending not to notice how offended she was, how bitterly stricken. He described the generous exchanges that would take place among the four of them abed. He asked whether she was getting excited. She said no, disgusted. Ah, you are but you won't give in to it, he said. His voice, his caresses grew more bullying. What is so special about you, he asked softly, despisingly, with a hard squeeze at her breasts. Georgia, why do you think you're such a queen?

"You are being cruel and you know you're being cruel," said Georgia, pulling at his hands. "Why are you being like this?"

"Honey, I'm not being cruel," said Miles, in a slippery mock-tender voice. "I'm being horny. I'm horny again is all." He began to pull Georgia around, to arrange her for his use. She told him to get out of the car.

"Squeamish," he said, in that same artificially and hatefully tender voice, as if he were licking fanatically at something loathsome. "You're a squeamish little slut."

Georgia told him that she would lean on the horn if he didn't stop. She would lean on the horn if he didn't get out of the car. She would yell for somebody to call the police. She did lean against the horn as they struggled. He pushed her away, with a whimpering curse such as she'd heard from him at other times, when it meant something different. He got out.

She could not believe that such ill will had erupted, that things had so stunningly turned around. When she thought of this afterward—a good long time afterward—she thought that perhaps he had acted for conscience' sake, to mark her off from Laura. Or to blot out what he had said to her last time. To humiliate her because he was frightened. Perhaps. Or perhaps all this seemed to him simply a further, and genuinely interesting, development in lovemaking.

She would have liked to talk it over with Maya. But the possibility of talking anything over with Maya had disappeared. Their friendship had come suddenly to an end.

The night after the incident at Clover Point, Georgia was sitting on the living-room floor playing a bedtime card game with her sons. The phone rang, and she was sure that it was Miles. She had been thinking all day that he would call, he would have to call to explain himself, to beg her pardon, to say that he had been testing her, in a way, or had been temporarily deranged by circumstances that she knew nothing about. She would not forgive him immediately. But she would not hang up.

It was Maya.

"Guess what weird thing happened," Maya said. "Miles phoned me. Your Miles. It's okay, Raymond isn't here. How did he even know my name?"

"I don't know," said Georgia.

She had told him it, of course. She had offered wild Maya up for his entertainment, or to point out what a novice at this game she herself was—a relatively chaste prize.

"He says he wants to come and talk to me," Maya said. "What do you think? What's the matter with him? Did you have a fight? . . . Yes? Oh, well, he probably wants me to persuade you to make up. I must say he picked the right night.

Raymond's at the hospital. He's got this balky woman in labor; he may have to stay and do a section on her. I'll phone and tell you how it goes. Shall I?"

After a couple of hours, with the children long asleep, Georgia began to expect Maya's call. She watched the television news, to take her mind off expecting it. She picked up the phone to make sure there was a dial tone. She turned off the television after the news, then turned it on again. She started to watch a movie; she watched it through three commercial breaks without going to the kitchen to look at the clock.

At half past midnight she went out and got into her car and drove to Maya's house. She had no idea what she would do there. And she did not do much of anything. She drove around the circular drive with the lights off. The house was dark. She could see that the garage was open and Raymond's car was not there. The motorcycle was nowhere in sight.

She had left her children alone, the doors unlocked. Nothing happened to them. They didn't wake up and discover her defection. No burglar, or prowler, or murderer surprised her on her return. That was a piece of luck that she did not even appreciate. She had gone out leaving the door open and the lights on, and when she came back she hardly recognized her folly, though she closed the door and turned out some lights and lay down on the living-room sofa. She didn't sleep. She lay still, as if the smallest movement would sharpen her suffering, until she saw the day getting light and heard the birds waking. Her limbs were stiff. She got up and went to the phone and listened again for the dial tone. She walked stiffly to the kitchen and put on the kettle and said to herself the words *a paralysis of grief.*

A paralysis of grief. What was she thinking of? That was what she would feel, how she might describe the way she would feel, if one of her children had died. Grief is for serious matters, important losses. She knew that. She would not have bartered away an hour of her children's lives to have had the phone ring at ten o'clock last night, to have heard Maya say, "Georgia, he's desperate. He's sorry; he loves you very much."

No. But it seemed that such a phone call would have given her a happiness that no look or word from her children could give her. Than anything could give her, ever again.

She phoned Maya before nine o'clock. As she was dialling, she thought that there were still some possibilities to pray for. Maya's phone had been temporarily out of order. Maya had been ill last night. Raymond had been in a car accident on his way home from the hospital.

All these possibilities vanished at the first sound of Maya's voice, which was sleepy (pretending to be sleepy?) and silky with deceit. "Georgia? Is that Georgia? Oh, I thought it was going to be Raymond. He had to stay over at the hospital in case this poor wretched woman needed a C-section. He was going to call me—"

"You told me that last night," said Georgia.

"He was going to call me—Oh, Georgia, I was supposed to call you! Now I remember. Yes. I was supposed to call you, but I thought it was probably too late. I thought the phone might wake up the children. I thought, Oh, better just leave it till morning!"

"How late was it?"

"Not awfully. I just thought."

"What happened?"

"What do you mean, what happened?" Maya laughed, like a lady in a silly play. "Georgia, are you in a state?"

"What happened?"

"Oh, Georgia," said Maya, groaning magnanimously but showing an edge of nerves. "Georgia, I'm sorry. It was nothing. It was just nothing. I've been rotten, but I didn't mean to be. I offered him a beer. Isn't that what you do when some-body rides up to your house on a motorcycle? You offer him a beer. But then he came on very lordly and said he only drank Scotch. And he said he'd only drink Scotch if I would drink with him. I thought he was pretty high-handed. Pretty high-handed pose. But I really was doing this for you, Georgia—I was wanting to find out what was on his mind. So I told him to put the motorcycle behind the garage, and I took him to sit in the back garden. That was so if I heard Raymond's car I could chase him out the back way and he could walk the motorcycle down the lane. I am not about to unload anything *new* onto Raymond at this point. I mean even something innocent, which this started out to be."

Georgia, with her teeth chattering, hung up the phone. She never spoke to Maya again. Maya appeared at her door, of course, a little while later, and Georgia had to let her in, because the children were playing in the yard. Maya sat down contritely at the kitchen table and asked if she could smoke. Georgia did not answer. Maya said she would smoke anyway and she hoped it was all right. Georgia pretended that Maya wasn't there. While Maya smoked, Georgia cleaned the stove, dismantling the elements and putting them back together again. She wiped the counters and polished the taps and straightened out the cutlery drawer. She mopped the floor around Maya's feet. She worked briskly, thoroughly, and never quite looked at Maya. At first she was not sure whether she could keep this up. But it got easier. The more earnest Maya became—the further she slipped from sensible remonstrance, half-amused confession, into true and fearful regret—the more fixed Georgia was in her resolve, the more grimly satisfied in her heart. She took care, however, not to appear grim. She moved about lightly. She was almost humming.

She took a knife to scrape out the grease from between the counter tiles by the stove. She had let things get into a bad way.

Maya smoked one cigarette after another, stubbing them out in a saucer that she fetched for herself from the cupboard. She said, "Georgia, this is so stupid. I can tell you, he's not worth it. It was nothing. All it was was Scotch and opportunity."

She said, "I am really sorry. Truly sorry. I know you don't believe me. How can I say it so you will?"

And, "Georgia, listen. You are humiliating me. Fine. Fine. Maybe I deserve it. I do deserve it. But after you've humiliated me enough we'll go back to being friends and we'll laugh about this. When we're old ladies, I swear we'll laugh. We won't be able to remember his name. We'll call him the motorcycle sheikh. We will."

Then, "Georgia, what do you want me to do? Do you want me to throw myself on the floor? I'm about ready to. I'm trying to keep myself from snivelling, and I can't. I'm snivelling, Georgia. Okay?"

She had begun to cry. Georgia put on her rubber gloves and started to clean the oven.

"You win," said Maya. "I'll pick up my cigarettes and go home."

She phoned a few times. Georgia hung up on her. Miles phoned, and Georgia hung up on him too. She thought he sounded cautious but smug. He phoned again and his voice trembled, as if he were striving just for candor and humility, bare love. Georgia hung up at once. She felt violated, shaken.

Maya wrote a letter, which said, in part, *I suppose you know that Miles is going back to Seattle and whatever home fires he keeps burning there. It seems the treasure thing has fallen through. But you must have known he was bound to go sometime and you'd have felt rotten then, so now you've got the rotten feeling over with. So isn't that okay? I don't say this to excuse myself. I know I was weak and putrid. But can't we put it behind us now?*

She went on to say that she and Raymond were going on a long-planned holiday to Greece and Turkey, and that she hoped very much that she would get a note from Georgia before she left. But if she didn't get any word she would try to understand what Georgia was telling her, and she would not make a nuisance of herself by writing again.

She kept her word. She didn't write again. She sent, from Turkey, a pretty piece of striped cloth large enough for a tablecloth. Georgia folded it up and put it away. She left it for Ben to find after she moved out, several months later.

"I'm happy," Raymond tells Georgia. "I'm very happy, and the reason is that I'm content to be an ordinary sort of person with an ordinary calm life. I am not looking for any big revelation or any big drama or any messiah of the opposite sex. I don't go around figuring out how to make things more interesting. I can say to you quite frankly I think Maya made a mistake. I don't mean she wasn't very gifted and intelligent and creative and so on, but she was looking for something—maybe she was looking for something that just is not there. And she tended to despise a lot that she had. It's true. She didn't want the privileges she had. We'd travel, for example, and she wouldn't want to stay in a comfortable hotel. No. She had to go on some trek that involved riding on poor, miserable donkeys and drinking sour milk for breakfast. I suppose I sound very square. Well, I suppose I am. I am square. You know, she had such beautiful silver. Magnificent silver. It was passed down through her family. And she couldn't be bothered to polish it or get the cleaning woman to polish it. She wrapped it all up in plastic and hid it away. She hid it away—you'd think it was a disgrace. How do you think she envisaged herself? As some kind of hippie, maybe? Some kind of free spirit? She didn't even realize it was her money that kept her afloat. I'll tell you, some of the free spirits I've seen pass in and out of this house wouldn't have been long around her without it.

"I did all I could," said Raymond. "I didn't scoot off and leave her, like her Prince of Fantasy Land."

Georgia got a vengeful pleasure out of breaking with Maya. She was pleased with the controlled manner in which she did it. The deaf ear. She was surprised to find herself capable of such control, such thoroughgoing punishment. She punished Maya. She punished Miles, through Maya, as much as she could. What she had to do, and she knew it, was to scrape herself raw, to root out all addiction to the gifts of those two pale prodigies. Miles and Maya. Both of them slippery, shimmery—liars, seducers, finaglers. But you would have thought that after such scourging she'd have scuttled back into her marriage and locked its doors, and appreciated what she had there as never before.

That was not what happened. She broke with Ben. Within a year, she was gone. Her way of breaking was strenuous and unkind. She told him about Miles, though she spared her own pride by leaving out the part about Miles and Maya. She took no care—she had hardly any wish—to avoid unkindness. On the night when she waited for Maya to call, some bitter, yeasty spirit entered into her. She saw herself as a person surrounded by, living by, sham. Because she had been so readily unfaithful, her marriage was a sham. Because she had gone so far out of it, so quickly, it was a sham. She dreaded, now, a life like Maya's.

She dreaded just as much a life like her own before this happened. She could not but destroy. Such cold energy was building in her she had to blow her own house down.

She had entered with Ben, when they were both so young, a world of ceremony, of safety, of gestures, concealment. Fond appearances. More than appearances. Fond contrivance. (She thought when she left that she would have no use for contrivance anymore.) She had been happy there, from time to time. She had been sullen, restless, bewildered, and happy. But she said most vehemently, Never, never. I was never happy, she said.

People always say that.

People make momentous shifts, but not the changes they imagine.

Just the same, Georgia knows that her remorse about the way she changed her life is dishonest. It is real and dishonest. Listening to Raymond, she knows that whatever she did she would have to do again. She would have to do it again, supposing that she had to be the person she was.

Raymond does not want to let Georgia go. He does not want to part with her. He offers to drive her downtown. When she has gone, he won't be able to talk about Maya. Very likely Anne has told him that she does not want to hear any more on the subject of Maya.

"Thank you for coming," he says on the doorstep. "Are you sure about the ride? Are you sure you can't stay to dinner?"

Georgia reminds him again about the bus, the last ferry. She says no, no, she really wants to walk. It's only a couple of miles. The late afternoon so lovely, Victoria so lovely. I had forgotten, she says.

Raymond says once more, "Thank you for coming."

"Thank you for the drinks," Georgia says. "Thank you too. I guess we never believe we are going to die."

"Now, now," says Raymond.

"No. I mean we never behave—we never behave as if we believed we were going to die."

Raymond smiles more and more and puts a hand on her shoulder. "How should we behave?" he says.

"Differently," says Georgia. She puts a foolish stress on the word, meaning that her answer is so lame that she can offer it only as a joke.

Raymond hugs her, then involves her in a long chilly kiss. He fastens onto her with an appetite that is grievous but unconvincing. A parody of passion, whose intention neither one of them, surely, will try to figure out.

She doesn't think about that as she walks back to town through the yellow-leafed streets with their autumn smells and silences. Past Clover Point, the cliffs crowned with broom bushes, the mountains across the water. The mountains of the Olympic Peninsula, assembled like a blatant backdrop, a cutout of rainbow tissue paper. She doesn't think about Raymond, or Miles, or Maya, or even Ben.

She thinks about sitting in the store in the evenings. The light in the street, the complicated reflections in the windows. The accidental clarity.

CARRIED AWAY

LETTERS

In the dining room of the Commercial Hotel, Louisa opened the letter that had arrived that day from overseas. She ate steak and potatoes, her usual meal, and drank a glass of wine. There were a few travellers in the room, and the dentist who ate there every night because he was a widower. He had shown an interest in her in the beginning but had told her he had never before seen a woman touch wine or spirits.

"It is for my health," said Louisa gravely.

The white tablecloths were changed every week and in the meantime were protected by oilcloth mats. In winter, the dining room smelled of these mats wiped by a kitchen rag, and of coal fumes from the furnace, and beef gravy and dried potatoes and onions—a smell not unpleasant to anybody coming in hungry from the cold. On each table was a little cruet stand with the bottle of brown sauce, the bottle of tomato sauce, and the pot of horseradish.

The letter was addressed to "The Librarian, Carstairs Public Library, Carstairs, Ontario." It was dated six weeks before—January 4, 1917.

Perhaps you will be surprised to hear from a person you don't know and that doesn't remember your name. I hope you are still the same Librarian though enough time has gone by that you could have moved on.

What has landed me here in Hospital is not too serious. I see worse all around me and get my mind off of all that by picturing things and wondering for instance if you are still there in the Library. If you are the one I mean, you are about of medium size or perhaps not quite, with light brownish hair. You came a few months before it was time for me to go in the Army following on Miss Tamblyn who had been there since I first became a user aged nine or ten. In her time the books were pretty much every which way, and it was as much as your life was worth to ask her for the least help or anything since she was quite a dragon. Then when you came what a change, it was all put into sections of Fiction and Non-Fiction and History and Travel and you got the magazines arranged in order and put out as soon as they arrived, not left to molder away till everything in them was stale. I felt gratitude but did not know how to say so. Also I wondered what brought you there, you were an educated person.

My name is Jack Agnew and my card is in the drawer. The last book I took out was very good—H. G. Wells, Mankind in the Making. *My education was to Second Form in High School, then I went into Douds as many did. I didn't join up right away when I was eighteen so you will not see me as a Brave Man. I am a person tending to have my own ideas always. My only relative in Carstairs, or anyplace, is my father Patrick Agnew. He works for Douds not at' the factory but at the house doing the gardening. He is a lone wolf even more than me and goes out to the country fishing every chance he gets. I write him a letter sometimes but I doubt if he reads it.*

After supper Louisa went up to the Ladies' Parlor on the second floor, and sat down at the desk to write her reply.

I am very glad to hear you appreciated what I did in the Library though it was just the normal organization, nothing special.

I am sure you would like to hear news of home, but I am a poor person for the job, being an outsider here. I do talk to people in the Library and in the hotel. The travellers in the hotel mostly talk about how business is (it is brisk if you can get the goods) and a little about sickness, and a lot about the War. There are rumors on rumors and opinions galore, which I'm sure would make you laugh if they didn't make you angry. I will not bother to write them down because I am sure there is a Censor reading this who would cut my letter to ribbons.

You ask how I came here. There is no interesting story. My parents are both dead. My father worked for Eaton's in Toronto in the Furniture Department, and after his death my mother worked there too in Linens. And I also worked there for a while in Books. Perhaps you could say Eaton's was our Douds. I graduated from Jarvis Collegiate. I had some sickness which put me in hospital for a long time, but I am quite well now. I had a great deal of time to read and my favorite authors are Thomas Hardy, who is accused of being gloomy but I think is very true to life—and Willa Cather. I just happened to be in this town when I heard the Librarian had died and I thought, perhaps that is the job for me.

A good thing your letter reached me today as I am about to be discharged from here and don't know if it would have been sent on to where I am going. I am glad you did not think my letter was too foolish.

If you run into my father or anybody you do not need to say anything about the fact we are writing to each other. It is nobody's business and I know there are plenty of people would laugh at me writing to the Librarian as they did at me going to the Library even, why give them the satisfaction?

I am glad to be getting out of here. So much luckier than some I

see that will never walk or have their sight and will have to hide
themselves away from the world.

You asked where did I live in Carstairs. Well, it was not anyplace to
be proud of. If you know where Vinegar Hill is and you turned off on
Flowers Road it is the last house on the right, yellow paint once upon
a time. My father grows potatoes, or did. I used to take them around
town with my wagon, and every load I sold got a nickel to keep.

You mention favorite authors. At one time I was fond of Zane
Grey, but I drifted away from reading fiction stories to reading History or Travel. I sometimes read books away over my head, I know,
but I do get something out of them. H. G. Wells I mentioned is one
and Robert Ingersoll who writes about religion. They have given me
a lot to think about. If you are very religious I hope I have not
offended you.

One day when I got to the Library it was a Saturday afternoon
and you had just unlocked the door and were putting the lights on
as it was dark and raining out. You had been caught out with no
hat or umbrella and your hair had got wet. You took the pins out of
it and let it come down. Is it too personal a thing to ask if you have
it long still or have you cut it? You went over and stood by the radiator and shook your hair on it and the water sizzled like grease in
the frying pan. I was sitting reading in the London Illustrated
News about the War. We exchanged a smile. (I didn't mean to say
your hair was greasy when I wrote that!)

I have not cut my hair though I often think about it. I do not know
if it is vanity or laziness that prevents me.

I am not very religious.

I walked up Vinegar Hill and found your house. The potatoes
are looking healthy. A police dog disputed with me, is he yours?

The weather is getting quite warm. We have had the flood on
the river, which I gather is an annual Spring event. The water got
into the hotel basement and somehow contaminated our drinking

*supply so that we were given free beer or ginger ale. But only if we
lived or were staying there. You can imagine there were plenty of
jokes.*

I should ask if there is anything that I could send you.

*I am not in need of anything particular. I get the tobacco and other
bits of things the ladies in Carstairs do up for us. I would like to
read some books by the authors you have mentioned but I doubt
whether I would get the chance here.*

*The other day there was a man died of a heart attack. It was the
News of all time. Did you hear about the man who died of a heart
attack? That was all you heard about day and night here. Then
everybody would laugh which seems hard-hearted but it just seemed
so strange. It was not even a hot time so you couldn't say maybe he
was scared. (As a matter of fact he was writing a letter at the time so
I had better look out.) Before and after him others have died being
shot up or blown up but he is the famous one, to die of a heart
attack. Everybody is saying what a long way to come and a lot of
expense for the Army to go to, for that.*

*The summer has been so dry the watering tank has been doing the
streets every day, trying to lay the dust. The children would dance
along behind it. There was also a new thing in town—a cart with a
little bell that went along selling ice cream, and the children were
pretty attentive to this as well. It was pushed by the man who had
an accident at the factory—you know who I mean, though I can't
recall his name. He lost his arm to the elbow. My room at the hotel,
being on the third floor, it was like an oven, and I often walked
about till after midnight. So did many other people, sometimes in
pajamas. It was like a dream. There was still a little water in the
river, enough to go out in a rowboat, and the Methodist minister did
that on a Sunday in August. He was praying for rain in a public
service. But there was a small leak in the boat and the water came in*

and wet his feet and eventually the boat sank and left him standing in the water, which did not nearly reach his waist. Was it an accident or a malicious trick? The talk was all that his prayers were answered but from the wrong direction.

I often pass the Douds' place on my walks. Your father keeps the lawns and hedges looking beautiful. I like the house, so original and airy-looking. But it may not have been cool even there, because I heard the voice of the mother and baby daughter late at night as if they were out on the lawn.

Though I told you there is nothing I need, there is one thing I would like. That is a photograph of you. I hope you will not think I am overstepping the bounds to ask for it. Maybe you are engaged to somebody or have a sweetheart over here you are writing to as well as me. You are a cut above the ordinary and it would not surprise me if some Officer had spoken for you. But now that I have asked I cannot take it back and will just leave it up to you to think what you like of me.

Louisa was twenty-five years old and had been in love once, with a doctor she had known in the sanitorium. Her love was returned, eventually, costing the doctor his job. There was some harsh doubt in her mind about whether he had been told to leave the sanitorium or had left of his own accord, being weary of the entanglement. He was married, he had children. Letters had played a part that time, too. After he left, they were still writing to one another. And once or twice after she was released. Then she asked him not to write anymore and he didn't. But the failure of his letters to arrive drove her out of Toronto and made her take the travelling job. Then there would be only the one disappointment in the week, when she got back on Friday or Saturday night. Her last letter had been firm and stoical, and some consciousness of herself as a heroine of love's tragedy went with her around the country as she hauled her display cases up and down the stairs of small hotels and talked about Paris styles and said that her sample hats were bewitching, and drank her solitary glass of wine. If she'd had anybody to tell, though, she would have laughed at just that notion. She would have said love was all hocus-pocus, a deception, and she believed that. But at the prospect she still felt a hush, a flutter along the nerves, a bowing down of sense, a flagrant prostration.

She had a picture taken. She knew how she wanted it to be. She would have liked to wear a simple white blouse, a peasant girl's smock with the string open at the neck. She did not own a blouse of that description and in fact had only seen them in pictures. And she would have liked to let her hair down. Or if it had to be up, she would have liked it piled very loosely and bound with strings of pearls.

Instead she wore her blue silk shirtwaist and bound her hair as usual. She thought the picture made her look rather pale, hollow-eyed. Her expression was sterner and more foreboding than she had intended. She sent it anyway.

I am not engaged, and do not have a sweetheart. I was in love once and it had to be broken off. I was upset at the time but I knew I must bear it, and now I believe that it was all for the best.

She had wracked her brains, of course, to remember him. She could not remember shaking out her hair, as he said she had done, or smiling at any young man when the raindrops fell on the radiator. He might as well have dreamed all that, and perhaps he had.

She had begun to follow the war in a more detailed way than she had done previously. She did not try to ignore it anymore. She went along the street with a sense that her head was filled with the same exciting and troubling information as everybody else's. Saint-Quentin, Arras, Montdidier, Amiens, and then there was a battle going on at the Somme River, where surely there had been one before? She laid open on her desk the maps of the war that appeared as double-page spreads in the magazines. She saw in colored lines the German drive to the Marne, the first thrust of the Americans at Château-Thierry. She looked at the artist's brown pictures of a horse rearing up during an air attack, of some soldiers in East Africa drinking out of coconuts, and of a line of German prisoners with bandaged heads or limbs and bleak, sullen expressions. Now she felt what everybody else did—a constant fear and misgiving and at the same time this addictive excitement. You could look up from your life of the moment and feel the world crackling beyond the walls.

I am glad to hear you do not have a sweetheart though I know that is selfish of me. I do not think you and I will ever meet again. I don't say that because I've had a dream about what will happen or am a gloomy person always looking for the worst. It just seems to me it is the most probable thing to happen, though I don't dwell on it and go along every day doing the best I can to stay alive. I am not trying to worry you or get your sympathy either but just explain how the idea I won't ever see Carstairs again makes me think I can say anything I want. I guess it's like being sick with a fever. So I will say I love you. I think of you up on a stool at the Library reaching to put a book away and I come up and put my hands on your waist and lift you down, and you turning around inside my arms as if we agreed about everything.

Every Tuesday afternoon the ladies and girls of the Red Cross met in the Council Chambers, which was just down the hall from the Library. When the Library was empty for a few moments, Louisa went down the hall and entered the room full of women. She had decided to knit a scarf. At the sanitorium she had learned how to knit a basic stitch, but she had never learned or had forgotten how to cast on or off.

The older women were all busy packing boxes or cutting up and folding bandages from sheets of heavy cotton that were spread on the tables. But a lot of girls near the door were eating buns and drinking tea. One was holding a skein of wool on her arms for another to wind.

Louisa told them what she needed to know.

"So what do you want to knit, then?" said one of the girls with some bun still in her mouth.

Louisa said, a muffler. For a soldier.

"Oh, you'll want the regulation wool," another said, more politely, and jumped off the table. She came back with some balls of brown wool, and fished a spare pair of needles out of her bag, telling Louisa they could be hers.

"I'll just get you started," she said. "It's a regulation width, too."

Other girls gathered around and teased this girl, whose name was Corrie. They told her she was doing it all wrong.

"Oh, I am, am I?" said Corrie. "How would you like a knitting needle in your eye? Is it for a friend?" she said solicitously to Louisa. "A friend overseas?"

"Yes," said Louisa. Of course they would think of her as an old maid, they would laugh at her or feel sorry for her, according to whatever show they put on, of being kind or brazen.

"So knit up good and tight," said the one who'd finished her bun. "Knit up good and tight to keep him warm!"

One of the girls in this group was Grace Horne. She was a shy but resolute-looking girl, nineteen years old, with a broad face, thin lips often pressed together, brown hair cut in a straight bang, and an attractively mature body. She had become engaged to Jack Agnew before he went overseas, but they had agreed not to say anything about it.

SPANISH FLU

Louisa had made friends with some of the travellers who stayed regularly at the hotel. One of these was Jim Frarey, who sold typewriters and office equipment and books and all sorts of stationery supplies. He was a fair-haired, rather round-shouldered but strongly built man in his middle forties. You would think by the look of him that he sold something heavier and more important in the masculine world, like farm implements.

Jim Frarey kept travelling all through the Spanish flu epidemic, though you never knew then if stores would be open for business or not. Occasionally the hotels, too, would be closed, like the schools and movie houses and even—Jim Frarey thought this a scandal—the churches.

"They ought to be ashamed of themselves, the cowards," he said to Louisa. "What good does it do anybody to lurk around home and wait for it to strike? Now you never closed the Library, did you?"

Louisa said only when she herself was sick. A mild case, hardly lasting a week, but of course she had to go to the hospital. They wouldn't let her stay in the hotel.

"Cowards," he said. "If you're going to be taken, you'll be taken. Don't you agree?"

They discussed the crush in the hospitals, the deaths of doctors and nurses, the unceasing drear spectacle of the funerals. Jim Frarey lived down the street from an undertaking establishment in Toronto. He said they still got out the black horses, the

black carriage, the works, to bury such personages as war-
ranted a fuss.

"Day and night they went on," he said. "Day and night." He
raised his glass and said, "Here's to health, then. You look well
yourself."

He thought that in fact Louisa was looking better than she
used to. Maybe she had started putting on rouge. She had a
pale-olive skin, and it seemed to him that her cheeks used to
be without color. She dressed with more dash, too, and took
more trouble to be friendly. She used to be very on-again, off-
again, just as she chose. She was drinking whisky, now, too,
though she would not try it without drowning it in water. It
used to be only a glass of wine. He wondered if it was a
boyfriend that had made the difference. But a boyfriend might
perk up her looks without increasing her interest in all and
sundry, which was what he was pretty sure had happened. It was
more likely time running out and the husband prospects thinned
out so dreadfully by the war. That could set a woman stirring.
She was smarter and better company and better-looking, too,
than most of the married ones. What happened with a woman
like that? Sometimes just bad luck. Or bad judgment at a time
when it mattered. A little too sharp and self-assured, in the old
days, making the men uneasy?

"Life can't be brought to a standstill all the same," he said.
"You did the right thing, keeping the Library open."

This was in the early winter of 1919, when there had been a
fresh outbreak of flu after the danger was supposed to be past.
They seemed to be all alone in the hotel. It was only about
nine o'clock but the hotelkeeper had gone to bed. His wife
was in the hospital with the flu. Jim Frarey had brought the
bottle of whisky from the bar, which was closed for fear of
contagion—and they sat at a table beside the window, in the
dining room. A winter fog had collected outside and was press-

ing against the window. You could barely see the streetlights or the few cars that trundled cautiously over the bridge.

"Oh, it was not a matter of principle," Louisa said. "That I kept the Library open. It was a more personal reason than you think."

Then she laughed and promised him a peculiar story. "Oh, the whisky must have loosened my tongue," she said.

"I am not a gossip," said Jim Frarey.

She gave him a hard laughing look and said that when a person announced they weren't a gossip, they almost invariably were. The same when they promised never to tell a soul.

"You can tell this where and when you like just as long as you leave out the real names and don't tell it around here," she said. "That I hope I can trust you not to do. Though at the moment I don't feel as if I cared. I'll probably feel otherwise when the drink wears off. It's a lesson, this story. It's a lesson in what fools women can make of themselves. So, you say, what's new about that, you can learn it every day!"

She began to tell him about a soldier who had started writing letters to her from overseas. The soldier remembered her from when he used to go into the Library. But she didn't remember him. However, she replied in a friendly way to his first letter and a correspondence sprang up between them. He told her where he had lived in the town and she walked past the house so that she could tell him how things looked there. He told her what books he'd read and she gave some of the same kind of information. In short, they both revealed something of themselves and feelings warmed up on either side. On his side first, as far as any declarations went. She was not one to rush in like a fool. At first, she thought she was simply being kind. Even later, she didn't want to reject and embarrass him. He asked for a picture. She had one taken, it was not to her liking, but she sent it. He asked if she had a sweetheart and she replied truthfully that she did not. He did not send any picture of himself nor did she ask for one, though of course she was curious as to what he looked like. It would be no easy matter for him to have a picture taken in the middle of a war. Furthermore, she did not want to seem like the sort of woman who would withdraw kindness if looks did not come up to scratch.

He wrote that he did not expect to come home. He said he was not so afraid of dying as he was of ending up like some of the men he had seen when he was in the hospital, wounded. He did not elaborate, but she supposed he meant the cases they were just getting to know about now—the stumps of men, the blinded, the ones made monstrous with burns. He was not whining about his fate, she did not mean to imply that. It was just that he expected to die and picked death over some other options and he thought about her and wrote to her as men do to a sweetheart in such a situation.

When the war ended, it was a while since she had heard from him. She went on expecting a letter every day and nothing came. Nothing came. She was afraid that he might have been one of those unluckiest of soldiers in the whole war— one of those killed in the last week, or on the last day, or even in the last hour. She searched the local paper every week, and the names of new casualties were still being printed there till after New Year's but his was not among them. Now the paper began to list as well the names of those returning home, often printing a photo with the name, and a little account of rejoicing. When the soldiers were returning thick and fast there was less room for these additions. And then she saw his name, another name on the list. He had not been killed, he had not been wounded—he was coming home to Carstairs, perhaps was already there.

It was then that she decided to keep the Library open, though the flu was raging. Every day she was sure he would come, every day she was prepared for him. Sundays were a torment. When she entered the Town Hall she always felt he might be there before her, leaning up against the wall awaiting her arrival. Sometimes she felt it so strongly she saw a shadow that she mistook for a man. She understood now how people believed they had seen ghosts. Whenever the door opened she expected to look up into his face. Sometimes she made a pact with herself not to look up till she had counted to ten. Few people came in, because of the flu. She set herself jobs of rearranging things, else she would have gone mad. She never locked up until five or ten minutes after closing time. And then she fancied that he might be across the street on the Post Office steps, watching her, being too shy to make a move. She worried of course that he might be ill, she always sought in conversation for news of the latest cases. No one spoke his name.

It was at this time that she entirely gave up on reading. The covers of books looked like coffins to her, either shabby or ornate, and what was inside them might as well have been dust.

She had to be forgiven, didn't she, she had to be forgiven for thinking, after such letters, that the one thing that could never happen was that he wouldn't approach her, wouldn't get in touch with her at all? Never cross her threshold, after such avowals? Funerals passed by her window and she gave no thought to them, as long as they were not his. Even when she was sick in the hospital her only thought was that she must get back, she must get out of bed, the door must not stay locked against him. She staggered to her feet and back to work. On a hot afternoon she was arranging fresh newspapers on the racks and his name jumped out at her like something in her feverish dreams.

She read a short notice of his marriage to a Miss Grace Horne. Not a girl she knew. Not a Library user.

The bride wore fawn silk crêpe with brown-and-cream piping, and a beige straw hat with brown velvet streamers.

There was no picture. Brown-and-cream piping. Such was the end, and had to be, to her romance.

But on her desk at the Library, a matter of a few weeks ago, on a Saturday night after everybody had gone and she had locked the door and was turning out the lights, she discovered a scrap of paper. A few words written on it. *I was engaged before I went overseas.* No name, not his or hers. And there was her photograph, partly shoved under the blotter.

He had been in the Library that very evening. It had been a busy time, she had often left the desk to find a book for somebody or to straighten up the papers or to put some books on the shelves. He had been in the same room with her, watched her, and taken his chance. But never made himself known.

I was engaged before I went overseas.

"Do you think it was all a joke on me?" Louisa said. "Do you think a man could be so diabolical?"

"In my experience, tricks like that are far more often indulged in by the women. No, no. Don't you think such a thing. Far more likely he was sincere. He got a little carried away. It's all just the way it looks on the surface. He was engaged before he went overseas, he never expected to get back in one piece but he did. And when he did, there is the fiancée waiting—what else could he do?"

"What indeed?" said Louisa.

"He bit off more than he could chew."

"Ah, that's so, that's so!" Louisa said. "And what was it in my case but vanity, which deserves to get slapped down!" Her eyes were glassy and her expression roguish. "You don't think he'd had a good look at me any one time and thought the original was even worse than that poor picture, so he backed off?"

"I do not!" said Jim Frarey. "And don't you so belittle yourself."

"I don't want you to think I am stupid," she said. "I am not so stupid and inexperienced as that story makes me sound."

"Indeed I don't think you are stupid at all."

"But perhaps you think I am inexperienced?"

This was it, he thought—the usual. Women after they have told one story on themselves cannot stop from telling another. Drink upsets them in a radical way, prudence is out the window.

She had confided in him once before that she had been a patient in a sanitorium. Now she told about being in love with a doctor there. The sanitorium was on beautiful grounds up on Hamilton Mountain, and they used to meet there along the hedged walks. Shelves of limestone formed the steps and in sheltered spots there were such plants as you do not commonly see in Ontario—azaleas, rhododendrons, magnolias. The doctor knew something about botany and he told her this was the Carolinian vegetation. Very different from here, lusher, and there were little bits of woodland, too, wonderful trees, paths worn under the trees. Tulip trees.

"Tulips!" said Jim Frarey. "Tulips on the trees!"

"No, no, it is the shape of their leaves!"

She laughed at him challengingly, then bit her lip. He saw fit to continue the dialogue, saying, "Tulips on the trees!" while she said no, it is the leaves that are shaped like tulips, no, I never said that, stop! So they passed into a state of gingerly evaluation—which he knew well and could only hope she did—full of small pleasant surprises, half-sardonic signals, a welling-up of impudent hopes, and a fateful sort of kindness.

"All to ourselves," Jim Frarey said. "Never happened before, did it? Maybe it never will again."

She let him take her hands, half lift her from her chair. He turned out the dining-room lights as they went out. Up the stairs they went, that they had so often climbed separately. Past the picture of the dog on his master's grave, and Highland Mary singing in the field, and the old King with his bulgy eyes, his look of indulgence and repletion.

"It's a foggy, foggy night, and my heart is in a fright," Jim Frarey was half singing, half humming as they climbed. He kept an assured hand on Louisa's back. "All's well, all's well," he said as he steered her round the turn of the stairs. And when they took the narrow flight of steps to the third floor he said, "Never climbed so close to Heaven in this place before!"

But later in the night Jim Frarey gave a concluding groan and roused himself to deliver a sleepy scolding. "Louisa, Louisa, why didn't you tell me that was the way it was?"

"I told you everything," said Louisa in a faint and drifting voice.

"I got a wrong impression, then," he said. "I never intended for this to make a difference to you."

She said that it hadn't. Now without him pinning her down and steadying her, she felt herself whirling around in an irresistible way, as if the mattress had turned into a child's top and was carrying her off. She tried to explain that the traces of blood on the sheets could be credited to her period, but her words came out with a luxurious nonchalance and could not be fitted together.

ACCIDENTS

When Arthur came home from the factory a little before noon he shouted, "Stay out of my way till I wash! There's been an accident over at the works!" Nobody answered. Mrs. Feare, the housekeeper, was talking on the kitchen telephone so loudly that she could not hear him, and his daughter was of course at school. He washed, and stuffed everything he had been wearing into the hamper, and scrubbed up the bathroom, like a murderer. He started out clean, with even his hair slicked and patted, to drive to the man's house. He had had to ask where it was. He thought it was up Vinegar Hill but they said no, that was the father—the young fellow and his wife live on the other side of town, past where the Apple Evaporator used to be, before the war.

He found the two brick cottages side by side, and picked the left-hand one, as he'd been told. It wouldn't have been hard to pick which house, anyway. News had come before him. The door to the house was open, and children too young to be in school yet hung about in the yard. A small girl sat on a kiddie car, not going anywhere, just blocking his path. He stepped around her. As he did so an older girl spoke to him in a formal way—a warning.

"Her dad's dead. Hers!"

A woman came out of the front room carrying an armload of curtains, which she gave to another woman standing in the hall. The woman who received the curtains was gray-haired, with a pleading face. She had no upper teeth. She probably took her plate out, for comfort, at home. The woman who passed the curtains to her was stout but young, with fresh skin.

"You tell her not to get up on that stepladder," the gray-haired woman said to Arthur. "She's going to break her neck taking down curtains. She thinks we need to get everything washed. Are you the undertaker? Oh, no, excuse me! You're Mr. Doud. Grace, come out here! Grace! It's Mr. Doud!"

"Don't trouble her," Arthur said.

"She thinks she's going to get the curtains all down and washed and up again by tomorrow, because he's going to have to go in the front room. She's my daughter. I can't tell her anything."

"She'll quiet down presently," said a somber but comfortable-looking man in a clerical collar, coming through from the back of the house. Their minister. But not from one of the churches Arthur knew. Baptist? Pentecostal? Plymouth Brethren? He was drinking tea.

Some other woman came and briskly removed the curtains. "We got the machine filled and going," she said. "A day like this, they'll dry like nobody's business. Just keep the kids out of here."

The minister had to stand aside and lift his teacup high, to avoid her and her bundle. He said, "Aren't any of you ladies going to offer Mr. Doud a cup of tea?"

Arthur said, "No, no, don't trouble.

"The funeral expenses," he said to the gray-haired woman. "if you could let her know—"

"Lillian wet her pants!" said a triumphant child at the door. "Mrs. Agnew! Lillian peed her pants!"

"Yes. Yes," said the minister. "They will be very grateful."

"The plot and the stone, everything," Arthur said. "You'll make sure they understand that. Whatever they want on the stone."

The gray-haired woman had gone out into the yard. She came back with a squalling child in her arms. "Poor lamb," she said. "They told her she wasn't supposed to come in the house so where could she go? What could she do but have an accident!"

The young woman came out of the front room dragging a rug.

"I want this put on the line and beat," she said.

"Grace, here is Mr. Doud come to offer his condolences," the minister said.

"And to ask if there is anything I can do," said Arthur.

The gray-haired woman started upstairs with the wet child in her arms and a couple of others following.

Grace spotted them.

"Oh, no, you don't! You get back outside!"

"My mom's in here."

"Yes and your mom's good and busy, she don't need to be bothered with you. She's here helping me out. Don't you know Lillian's dad's dead?"

"Is there anything I can do for you?" Arthur said, meaning to clear out.

Grace stared at him with her mouth open. Sounds of the washing machine filled the house.

"Yes, there is," she said. "You wait here."

"She's overwhelmed," the minister said. "It's not that she means to be rude."

Grace came back with a load of books.

"These here," she said. "He had them out of the Library. I don't want to have to pay fines on them. He went every Saturday night so I guess they are due back tomorrow. I don't want to get in trouble about them."

"I'll look after them," Arthur said. "I'd be glad to."

"I just don't want to get in any trouble about them."

"Mr. Doud was saying about taking care of the funeral," the minister said to her, gently admonishing. "Everything including the stone. Whatever you want on the stone."

"Oh, I don't want anything fancy," Grace said.

On Friday morning last there occurred in the sawmill operation of Douds Factory a particularly ghastly and tragic accident. Mr. Jack Agnew, in reaching under the main shaft, had the misfortune to have his sleeve caught by a setscrew in an adjoining flunge, so that his arm and shoulder were drawn under the shaft. His head in consequence was brought in contact with the circular saw, that saw being about one foot in diameter. In an instant the unfortunate young man's head was separated from his body, being severed at an angle below the

left ear and through the neck. His death is believed to have
been instantaneous. He never spoke or uttered a cry so it was
not any sound of his but by the spurt and shower of his blood
that his fellow-workers were horribly alerted to the disaster.

This account was reprinted in the paper a week later for
those who might have missed it or who wished to have an
extra copy to send to friends or relations out of town (particularly to people who used to live in Carstairs and did not anymore). The misspelling of "flange" was corrected. There was a
note apologizing for the mistake. There was also a description
of a very large funeral, attended even by people from neigh-
boring towns and as far away as Walley. They came by car and
train, and some by horse and buggy. They had not known Jack
Agnew when he was alive, but, as the paper said, they wished
to pay tribute to the sensational and tragic manner of his death.
All the stores in Carstairs were closed for two hours that afternoon. The hotel did not close its doors but that was because all
the visitors needed somewhere to eat and drink.

The survivors were a wife, Grace, and a four-year-old
daughter, Lillian. The victim had fought bravely in the Great
War and had only been wounded once, not seriously. Many
had commented on this irony.

The paper's failure to mention a surviving father was not
deliberate. The editor of the paper was not a native of Carstairs,
and people forgot to tell him about the father until it was too
late.

The father himself did not complain about the omission.
On the day of the funeral, which was very fine, he headed out
of town as he would have done ordinarily on a day he had
decided not to spend at Douds. He was wearing a felt hat and a
long coat that would do for a rug if he wanted to take a nap.

His overshoes were neatly held on his feet with the rubber rings from sealing jars. He was going out to fish for suckers. The season hadn't opened yet, but he always managed to be a bit ahead of it. He fished through the spring and early summer and cooked and ate what he caught. He had a frying pan and a pot hidden out on the riverbank. The pot was for boiling corn that he snatched out of the fields later in the year, when he was also eating the fruit of wild apple trees and grapevines. He was quite sane but abhorred conversation. He could not altogether avoid it in the weeks following his son's death, but he had a way of cutting it short.

"Should've watched out what he was doing."

Walking in the country that day, he met another person who was not at the funeral. A woman. She did not try to start any conversation and in fact seemed as fierce in her solitude as himself, whipping the air past her with long fervent strides.

The piano factory, which had started out making pump organs, stretched along the west side of town, like a medieval town wall. There were two long buildings like the inner and outer ramparts, with a closed-in bridge between them where the main offices were. And reaching up into the town and the streets of workers' houses you had the kilns and the sawmill and the lumberyard and storage sheds. The factory whistle dictated the time for many to get up, blowing at six o'clock in the morning. It blew again for work to start at seven and at twelve for dinnertime and at one in the afternoon for work to recommence, and then at five-thirty for the men to lay down their tools and go home.

Rules were posted beside the time clock, under glass. The first two rules were:

ONE MINUTE LATE IS FIFTEEN MINUTES PAY. BE PROMPT.
DON'T TAKE SAFETY FOR GRANTED. WATCH OUT
FOR YOURSELF AND THE NEXT MAN.

There had been accidents in the factory and in fact a man had been killed when a load of lumber fell on him. That had happened before Arthur's time. And once, during the war, a man had lost an arm, or part of an arm. On the day that happened, Arthur was away in Toronto. So he had never seen an accident—nothing serious, anyway. But it was often at the back of his mind now that something might happen.

Perhaps he did not feel so sure that trouble wouldn't come near him, as he had felt before his wife died. She had died in 1919, in the last flurry of the Spanish flu, when everyone had got over being frightened. Even she had not been frightened. That was nearly five years ago and it still seemed to Arthur like the end of a carefree time in his life. But to other people he had always seemed very responsible and serious—nobody had noticed much difference in him.

In his dreams of an accident there was a spreading silence, everything was shut down. Every machine in the place stopped making its customary noise and every man's voice was removed, and when Arthur looked out of the office window he understood that doom had fallen. He never could remember any particular thing he saw that told him this. It was just the space, the dust in the factory yard, that said to him *now.*

The books stayed on the floor of his car for a week or so. His daughter Bea said, "What are those books doing here?" and then he remembered.

Bea read out the titles and the authors. *Sir John Franklin and the Romance of the Northwest Passage*, by G. B. Smith. *What's Wrong with the World?*, G. K. Chesterton. *The Taking of Quebec*, Archibald Hendry. *Bolshevism: Practice and Theory*, by Lord Bertrand Russell.

"Bol-*shev*-ism," Bea said, and Arthur told her how to pronounce it correctly. She asked what it was, and he said, "It's something they've got in Russia that I don't understand so well myself. But from what I hear of it, it's a disgrace."

Bea was thirteen at this time. She had heard about the Russian Ballet and also about dervishes. She believed for the next couple of years that Bolshevism was some sort of diabolical and maybe indecent dance. At least this was the story she told when she was grown up.

She did not mention that the books were connected with the man who had had the accident. That would have made the story less amusing. Perhaps she had really forgotten.

The Librarian was perturbed. The books still had their cards in them, which meant they had never been checked out, just removed from the shelves and taken away.

"The one by Lord Russell has been missing a long time."

Arthur was not used to such reproofs, but he said mildly, "I am returning them on behalf of somebody else. The chap who was killed. In the accident at the factory."

The Librarian had the Franklin book open. She was looking at the picture of the boat trapped in the ice.

"His wife asked me to," Arthur said.

She picked up each book separately, and shook it as if she expected something to fall out. She ran her fingers in between the pages. The bottom part of her face was working in an unsightly way, as if she was chewing at the inside of her cheeks.

"I guess he just took them home as he felt like it," Arthur said.

"I'm sorry?" she said in a minute. "What did you say? I'm sorry."

It was the accident, he thought. The idea that the man who had died in such a way had been the last person to open these books, turn these pages. The thought that he might have left a bit of his life in them, a scrap of paper or a pipe cleaner as a marker, or even a few shreds of tobacco. That unhinged her.

"No matter," he said. "I just dropped by to bring them back."

He turned away from her desk but did not immediately leave the Library. He had not been in it for years. There was his father's picture between the two front windows, where it would always be.

A. V. Doud, founder of the Doud Organ Factory
and Patron of this Library. A Believer in Progress,
Culture, and Education. A True Friend of the Town
of Carstairs and of the Working Man.

The Librarian's desk was in the archway between the front and back rooms. The books were on shelves set in rows in the back room. Green-shaded lamps, with long pull cords, dangled down in the aisles between. Arthur remembered years ago some matter brought up at the Council Meeting about buying sixty-watt bulbs instead of forty. This Librarian was the one who had requested that, and they had done it.

In the front room, there were newspapers and magazines on wooden racks, and some round heavy tables, with chairs, so that people could sit and read, and rows of thick dark books behind glass. Dictionaries, probably, and atlases and encyclopedias. Two handsome high windows looking out on the main street, with Arthur's father hanging between them. Other pictures around the room hung too high, and were too dim and crowded with figures for the person down below to interpret them easily. (Later, when Arthur had spent many hours in the Library and had discussed these pictures with the Librarian, he knew that one of them represented the Battle of Flodden Field, with the King of Scotland charging down the hill into a pall of smoke, one the funeral of the Boy King of Rome, and one the Quarrel of Oberon and Titania, from *A Midsummer Night's Dream*.)

He sat down at one of the reading tables, where he could look out the window. He picked up an old copy of the *National Geographic*, which was lying there. He had his back to the Librarian. He thought this the tactful thing to do, since she seemed somewhat wrought-up. Other people came in, and he heard her speak to them. Her voice sounded normal enough now. He kept thinking he would leave, but did not.

He liked the high bare window full of the light of the spring evening, and he liked the dignity and order of these rooms. He was pleasantly mystified by the thought of grown people coming and going here, steadily reading books. Week after week, one book after another, a whole life long. He himself read a book once in a while, when somebody recommended it, and usually he enjoyed it, and then he read magazines, to keep up with things, and never thought about reading a book until another one came along, in this almost accidental way.

There would be little spells when nobody was in the Library but himself and the Librarian.

During one of these, she came over and stood near him, replacing some newspapers on the rack. When she finished this, she spoke to him, with a controlled urgency.

"The account of the accident that was printed in the paper—I take it that was more or less accurate?"

Arthur said that it was possibly too accurate.

"Why? Why do you say that?"

He mentioned the public's endless appetite for horrific details. Ought the paper to pander to that?

"Oh, I think it's natural," the Librarian said. "I think it's natural to want to know the worst. People do want to picture it. I do myself. I am very ignorant of machinery. It's hard for me to imagine what happened. Even with the paper's help. Did the machine do something unexpected?"

"No," Arthur said. "It wasn't the machine grabbing him and pulling him in, like an animal. He made a wrong move or at any rate a careless move. Then he was done for."

She said nothing, but did not move away.

"You have to keep your wits about you," Arthur said. "Never let up for a second. A machine is your servant and it is an excellent servant, but it makes an imbecile master."

He wondered if he had read that somewhere, or had thought it up himself.

"And I suppose there are no ways of protecting people?" the Librarian said. "But you must know all about that."

She left him then. Somebody had come in.

The accident was followed by a rush of warm weather. The length of the evenings and the heat of the balmy days seemed sudden and surprising, as if this were not the way winter finally ended in that part of the country, almost every year. The sheets of floodwater shrank magically back into the bogs, and the leaves shot out of the reddened branches, and barnyard smells drifted into town and were wrapped in the smell of lilacs.

Instead of wanting to be outdoors on such evenings, Arthur found himself thinking of the Library, and he would often end up there, sitting in the spot he had chosen on his first visit. He would sit for half an hour, or an hour. He looked at the London *Illustrated News*, or the *National Geographic* or *Saturday Night* or *Collier's*. All of these magazines arrived at his own house and he could have been sitting there, in the den, looking out at his hedged lawns, which old Agnew kept in tolerable condition, and the flower beds now full of tulips of every vivid color and combination. It seemed that he preferred the view of the main street, where the occasional brisk-looking new Ford went by, or some stuttering older-model car with a dusty cloth top. He preferred the Post Office, with its clock tower telling four different times in four different directions—and, as people liked to say, all wrong. Also the passing and loitering on the sidewalk. People trying to get the drinking fountain to work, although it wasn't turned on till the First of July.

It was not that he felt the need of sociability. He was not there for chat, though he would greet people if he knew them by name, and he did know most. And he might exchange a few words with the Librarian, though often it was only "Good evening" when he came in, and "Good night" when he went out. He made no demands on anybody. He felt his presence to be genial, reassuring, and, above all, natural. By sitting here, reading and reflecting, here instead of at home, he seemed to himself to be providing something. People could count on it.

There was an expression he liked. *Public servant.* His father, who looked out at him here with tinted baby-pink cheeks and glassy blue eyes and an old man's petulant mouth, had never thought of himself so. He had thought of himself more as a public character and benefactor. He had operated by whims and decrees, and he had got away with it. He would go around the factory when business was slow, and say to one man and another, "Go home. Go on home now. Go home and stay there till I can use you again." And they would go. They would work in their gardens or go out shooting rabbits and run up bills for whatever they had to buy, and accept that it couldn't be otherwise. It was still a joke with them, to imitate his bark. *Go on home!* He was their hero more than Arthur could ever be, but they were not prepared to take the same treatment today. During the war, they had got used to the good wages and to being always in demand. They never thought of the glut of labor the soldiers had created when they came home, never thought about how a business like this was kept going by luck and ingenuity from one year to the next, even from one season to the next. They didn't like changes—they were not happy about the switch now to player pianos, which Arthur believed were the hope of the future. But Arthur would do what he had to, though his way of proceeding was quite the opposite of his father's. Think everything over and then think it over again. Stay in the background except when necessary. Keep your dignity. Try always to be fair.

They expected all to be provided. The whole town expected it. Work would be provided just as the sun would rise in the mornings. And the taxes on the factory raised at the same time rates were charged for the water that used to come free. Maintenance of the access roads was now the factory's responsibility instead of the town's. The Methodist Church was requesting a hefty sum to build the new Sunday school. The town hockey team needed new uniforms. Stone gateposts were being erected for the War Memorial Park. And every year the smartest boy in the senior class was sent to university, courtesy of Douds.

Ask and ye shall receive.

Expectations at home were not lacking either. Bea was agitating to go away to private school and Mrs. Feare had her eye on some new mixing apparatus for the kitchen, also a new washing machine. All the trim on the house was due to be painted this year. All that wedding-cake decoration that consumed paint by the gallon. And in the midst of this what had Arthur done but order himself a new car—a Chrysler sedan.

It was necessary—he had to drive a new car. He had to drive a new car, Bea had to go away to school, Mrs. Feare had to have the latest, and the trim had to be as fresh as Christmas snow. Else they would lose respect, they would lose confidence, they would start to wonder if things were going downhill. And it could be managed, with luck it could all be managed.

For years after his father's death, he had felt like an impostor. Not steadily, but from time to time he had felt that. And now the feeling was gone. He could sit here and feel that it was gone.

He had been in the office when the accident happened, consulting with a veneer salesman. Some change in noise registered with him, but it was more of an increase than a hush. It was nothing that alerted him—just an irritation. Because it happened in the sawmill, nobody would know about the accident immediately in the shops or in the kilns or in the yard, and work in some places continued for several minutes. In fact Arthur, bending over the veneer samples on his desk, might have been one of the last people to understand that there had been an intervention. He asked the salesman a question, and the salesman did not answer. Arthur looked up and saw the man's mouth open, his face frightened, his salesman's assurance wiped away.

Then he heard his own name being called— both "Mr. Doud!" as was customary and "Arthur, Arthur!" by such of the older men as had known him as a boy. Also he heard "saw" and "head" and "Jesus, Jesus, Jesus!"

Arthur could have wished for the silence, the sounds and objects drawing back in that dreadful but releasing way, to give him room. It was nothing like that. Yelling and questioning and running around, himself in the midst being propelled to the sawmill. One man had fainted, falling in such a way that if they had not got the saw turned off a moment before, it would have got him, too. It was his body, fallen but entire, that Arthur briefly mistook for the body of the victim. Oh, no, no. They pushed him on. The sawdust was scarlet. It was drenched, brilliant. The pile of lumber here was all merrily spattered, and the blades. A pile of work clothes soaked in blood lay in the sawdust and Arthur realized that it was the body, the trunk with limbs attached. So much blood had flowed as to make its shape not plain at first—to soften it, like a pudding.

The first thing he thought of was to cover that. He took off his jacket and did so. He had to step up close, his shoes squished in it. The reason no one else had done this would be simply that no one else was wearing a jacket.

"Have they gone a-get the doctor?" somebody was yelling. "Gone a-get the doctor!" a man quite close to Arthur said. "Can't sew his head back on—doctor. Can he?"

But Arthur gave the order to get the doctor; he imagined it was necessary. You can't have a death without a doctor. That set the rest in motion. Doctor, undertaker, coffin, flowers, preacher. Get started on all that, give them something to do. Shovel up the sawdust, clean up the saw. Send the men who had been close by to wash themselves. Carry the man who had fainted to the lunchroom. Is he all right? Tell the office girl to make tea.

Brandy was what was needed, or whisky. But he had a rule against it, on the premises.

Something still lacking. Where was it? There, they said. Over there. Arthur heard the sound of vomiting, not far away. All right. Either pick it up or tell somebody to pick it up. The sound of vomiting saved him, steadied him, gave him an almost lighthearted determination. He picked it up. He carried it delicately and securely as you might carry an awkward but valuable jug. Pressing the face out of sight, as if comforting it, against his chest. Blood seeped through his shirt and stuck the material to his skin. Warm. He felt like a wounded man. He was aware of them watching him and he was aware of himself as an actor must be, or a priest. What to do with it, now that he had it against his chest? The answer to that came, too. Set it down, put it back where it belongs, not of course fitted with exactness, not as if a seam could be closed. Just more or less in place, and lift the jacket and tug it into a new position.

He couldn't now ask the man's name. He would have to get it in some other way. After the intimacy of his services here, such ignorance would be an offense.

But he found he did know it—it came to him. As he edged the corner of his jacket over the ear that had lain and still lay upward, and so looked quite fresh and usable, he received a name. Son of the fellow who came and did the garden, who was not always reliable. A young man taken on again when he came back from the war. Married? He thought so. He would have to go and see her. As soon as possible. Clean clothes.

The Librarian often wore a dark-red blouse. Her lips were reddened to match, and her hair was bobbed. She was not a young woman anymore, but she maintained an eye-catching style. He remembered that years ago when they had hired her, he had thought that she got herself up very soberly. Her hair was not bobbed in those days—it was wound around her head, in the old style. It was still the same color—a warm and pleasant color, like leaves—oak leaves, say, in the fall. He tried to think how much she was paid. Not much, certainly. She kept herself looking well on it. And where did she live? In one of the boarding houses—the one with the schoolteachers? No, not there. She lived in the Commercial Hotel.

And now something else was coming to mind. No definite story that he could remember. You could not say with any assurance that she had a bad reputation. But it was not quite a spotless reputation, either. She was said to take a drink with the travellers. Perhaps she had a boyfriend among them. A boyfriend or two.

Well, she was old enough to do as she liked. It wasn't quite the same as the way it was with a teacher—hired partly to set an example. As long as she did her job well, and anybody could see that she did. She had her life to live, like everyone else. Wouldn't you rather have a nice-looking woman in here than a crabby old affair like Mary Tamblyn? Strangers might drop in, they judge a town by what they see, you want a nice-looking woman with a nice manner.

Stop that. Who said you didn't? He was arguing in his head on her behalf just as if somebody had come along who wanted her chucked out, and he had no intimation at all that that was the case.

What about her question, on the first evening, regarding the machines? What did she mean by that? Was it a sly way of bringing blame?

He had talked to her about the pictures and the lighting and even told her how his father had sent his own workmen over here, paid them to build the Library shelves, but he had never spoken of the man who had taken the books out without letting her know. One at a time, probably. Under his coat? Brought back the same way. He must have brought them back, or else he'd have had a houseful, and his wife would never stand for that. Not stealing, except temporarily. Harmless behavior, but peculiar. Was there any connection? Between thinking you could do things a little differently that way and thinking you could get away with a careless move that might catch your sleeve and bring the saw down on your neck?

There might be, there might be some connection. A matter of attitude.

"That chap—you know the one—the accident—" he said

to the Librarian. "The way he took off with the books he wanted. Why do you think he did that?"

"People do things," the Librarian said. "They tear out pages. On account of something they don't like or something they do. They just do things. I don't know."

"Did he ever tear out some pages? Did you ever give him a lecture? Ever make him scared to face you?"

He meant to tease her a little, implying that she would not be likely to scare anybody, but she did not take it that way.

"How could I when I never spoke to him?" she said. "I never saw him. I never saw him, to know who he was."

She moved away, putting an end to the conversation. So she did not like to be teased. Was she one of those people full of mended cracks that you could only see close up? Some old misery troubling her, some secret? Maybe a sweetheart had been lost in the war.

On a later evening, a Saturday evening in the summer, she brought the subject up herself, that he would never have mentioned again.

"Do you remember our talking once about the man who had the accident?"

Arthur said he did.

"I have something to ask you and you may think it strange."

He nodded.

"And my asking it—I want you to—it is confidential."

"Yes, indeed," he said.

"What did he look like?"

Look like? Arthur was puzzled. He was puzzled by her making such a fuss and secret about it—surely it was natural to be interested in what a man might look like, who had been coming in and making off with her books without her knowing about it—and because he could not help her, he shook his head. He could not bring any picture of Jack Agnew to mind.

"Tall," he said. "I believe he was on the tall side. Otherwise I cannot tell you. I am really not such a good person to ask. I can recognize a man easily but I can't ever give much of a physical description, even when it's someone I see on a daily basis."

"But I thought you were the one—I heard you were the one—" she said. "Who picked him up. His head."

Arthur said stiffly, "I didn't think that you could just leave it lying there." He felt disappointed in the woman, uneasy and ashamed for her. But he tried to speak matter-of-factly, keeping reproach out of his voice.

"I could not even tell you the color of his hair. It was all—all pretty much obliterated, by that time."

She said nothing for a moment or two and he did not look at her. Then she said, "It must seem as if I am one of those people—one of those people who are fascinated by these sorts of things."

Arthur made a protesting noise, but it did, of course, seem to him that she must be like that.

"I should not have asked you," she said. "I should not have mentioned it. I can never explain to you why I did. I would like just to ask you, if you can help it, never to think that that is the kind of person I am."

Arthur heard the word "never." She could never explain to him. He was never to think. In the midst of his disappointment he picked up this suggestion, that their conversations were to continue, and perhaps on a less haphazard basis. He heard a humility in her voice, but it was a humility that was based on some kind of assurance. Surely that was sexual.

Or did he only think so, because this was the evening it was? It was the Saturday evening in the month when he usually went to Walley. He was going there tonight, he had only dropped in here on his way, he had not meant to stay as long as he had done. It was the night when he went to visit a woman whose name was Jane MacFarlane. Jane MacFarlane lived apart from her husband, but she was not thinking of getting a divorce. She had no children. She earned her living as a dressmaker. Arthur had first met her when she came to his house to make clothes for his wife. Nothing had gone on at that time, and neither of them had thought of it. In some ways Jane MacFarlane was a woman like the Librarian—good-looking, though not so young, plucky and stylish and good at her work. In other ways, not so like. He could not imagine Jane ever presenting a man with a mystery, and following that up with the information that it would never be solved. Jane was a woman to give a man peace. The submerged dialogue he had with her—sensual, limited, kind—was very like the one he had had with his wife.

The Librarian went to the switch by the door, and turned out the main light. She locked the door. She disappeared among the shelves, turning out the lights there, too, in a leisurely way. The town clock was striking nine. She must think that it was right. His own watch said three minutes to.

It was time to get up, time for him to leave, time to go to Walley.

When she had finished dealing with the lights, she came and sat down at the table beside him.

He said, "I would never think of you in any way that would make you unhappy."

Turning out the lights shouldn't have made it so dark. They were in the middle of summer. But it seemed that heavy rain clouds had moved in. When Arthur had last paid attention to the street, he had seen plenty of daylight left: country people shopping, boys squirting each other at the drinking fountain, and young girls walking up and down in their soft, cheap, flowery summer dresses, letting the young men watch them from wherever the young men congregated—the Post Office steps, the front of the feed store. And now that he looked again he saw the street in an uproar from the loud wind that already carried a few drops of rain. The girls were shrieking and laughing and holding their purses over their heads as they ran to shelter, store clerks were rolling up awnings and hauling in the baskets of fruit, the racks of summer shoes, the garden implements that had been displayed on the sidewalks. The doors of the Town Hall banged as the farm women ran inside, grabbing on to packages and children, to cram themselves into the Ladies' Rest Room. Somebody tried the Library door. The Librarian looked over at it but did not move. And soon the rain was sweeping like curtains across the street, and the wind battered the Town Hall roof, and tore at the treetops. That roaring and danger lasted a few minutes, while the power of the wind went by. Then the sound left was the sound of the rain, which was now falling vertically and so heavily they might have been under a waterfall.

If the same thing was happening at Walley, he thought, Jane would know enough not to expect him. This was the last thought he had of her for a long while.

"Mrs. Feare wouldn't wash my clothes," he said, to his own surprise. "She was afraid to touch them."

The Librarian said, in a peculiarly quivering, shamed, and determined voice, "I think what you did—I think that was a remarkable thing to do."

The rain made such a constant noise that he was released from answering. He found it easy then to turn and look at her. Her profile was dimly lit by the wash of rain down the windows. Her expression was calm and reckless. Or so it seemed to him. He realized that he knew hardly anything about her— what kind of person she really was or what kind of secrets she could have. He could not even estimate his own value to her. He only knew that he had some, and it wasn't the usual.

He could no more describe the feeling he got from her than you can describe a smell. It's like the scorch of electricity. It's like burnt kernels of wheat. No, it's like a bitter orange. I give up.

He had never imagined that he would find himself in a situation like this, visited by such a clear compulsion. But it seemed he was not unprepared. Without thinking over twice or even once what he was letting himself in for, he said, "I wish—"

He had spoken too quietly, she did not hear him.

He raised his voice. He said, "I wish we could get married."

Then she looked at him. She laughed but controlled herself.

"I'm sorry," she said. "I'm sorry. It's just what went through my mind."

"What was that?" he said.

"I thought—that's the last I'll see of him."

Arthur said, "You're mistaken."

TOLPUDDLE MARTYRS

The passenger train from Carstairs to London had stopped running during the Second World War and even the rails were taken up. People said it was for the War Effort. When Louisa went to London to see the heart specialist, in the mid-fifties, she had to take the bus. She was not supposed to drive anymore.

The doctor, the heart specialist, said that her heart was a little wonky and her pulse inclined to be jumpy. She thought that made her heart sound like a comedian and her pulse like a puppy on a lead. She had not come fifty-seven miles to be treated with such playfulness but she let it pass, because she was already distracted by something she had been reading in the

doctor's waiting room. Perhaps it was what she had been reading that had made her pulse jumpy.

On an inside page of the local paper she had seen the head-
line LOCAL MARTYRS HONORED, and simply to put in the time
she had read further. She read that there was to be some sort of
ceremony that afternoon at Victoria Park. It was a ceremony to
honor the Tolpuddle Martyrs. The paper said that few people
had heard of the Tolpuddle Martyrs, and certainly Louisa had
not. They were men who had been tried and found guilty for
administering illegal oaths. This peculiar offense, committed
over a hundred years ago in Dorset, England, had got them
transported to Canada and some of them had ended up here in
London, where they lived out the rest of their days and were
buried without any special notice or commemoration. They
were considered now to be among the earliest founders of the
Trade Union movement, and the Trade Unions Council, along
with representatives of the Canadian Federation of Labor and
the ministers of some local churches, had organized a ceremony taking place today on the occasion of the hundred-and-
twentieth anniversary of their arrest.

Martyrs is laying it on somewhat, thought Louisa. They were
not executed, after all.

The ceremony was to take place at three o'clock and the
chief speakers were to be one of the local ministers, and Mr.
John (Jack) Agnew, a union spokesman from Toronto.

It was a quarter after two when Louisa came out of the doctor's office. The bus to Carstairs did not leave until six o'clock.
She had thought she would go and have tea and something to
eat on the top floor of Simpsons, then shop for a wedding
present, or if the time fitted go to an afternoon movie. Victoria
Park lay between the doctor's office and Simpsons, and she
decided to cut across it. The day was hot and the shade of the
trees pleasant. She could not avoid seeing where the chairs had

been set up, and a small speakers' platform draped in yellow cloth, with a Canadian flag on the one side and what she supposed must be a Labor Union flag on the other. A group of people had collected and she found herself changing course in order to get a look at them. Some were old people, very plainly but decently dressed, the women with kerchiefs around their heads on the hot day, Europeans. Others were factory workers, men in clean short-sleeved shirts and women in fresh blouses and slacks, let out early. A few women must have come from home, because they were wearing summer dresses and sandals and trying to keep track of small children. Louisa thought that they would not care at all for the way she was dressed—fashionably, as always, in beige shantung with a crimson silk tam— but she noticed, just then, a woman more elegantly got up than she was, in green silk with her dark hair drawn tightly back, tied with a green-and-gold scarf. She might have been forty—her face was worn, but beautiful. She came over to Louisa at once, smiling, showed her a chair and gave her a mimeographed paper. Louisa could not read the purple printing. She tried to get a look at some men who were talking beside the platform. Were the speakers among them?

The coincidence of the name was hardly even interesting. Neither the first name nor the last was all that unusual.

She did not know why she had sat down, or why she had come over here in the first place. She was beginning to feel a faintly sickening, familiar agitation. She could feel that over nothing. But once it got going, telling herself that it was over nothing did no good. The only thing to do was to get up and get away from here before any more people sat down and hemmed her in.

The green woman intercepted her, asked if she was all right.

"I have to catch a bus," said Louisa in a croaky voice. She cleared her throat. "An out-of-town bus," she said with better control, and marched away, not in the right direction for Simpsons. She thought in fact that she wouldn't go there, she wouldn't go to Birks for the wedding present or to a movie either. She would just go and sit in the bus depot until it was time for her to go home.

Within half a block of the bus depot she remembered that the bus had not taken her there that morning. The depot was being torn down and rebuilt—there was a temporary depot several blocks away. She had not paid quite enough attention to which street it was on—York Street, east of the real depot, or King? At any rate, she had to detour, because both of these streets were being torn up, and she had almost decided she was lost when she realized she had been lucky enough to come upon the temporary depot by the back way. It was an old house—one of those tall yellow-gray brick houses dating from the time when this was a residential district. This was probably the last use it would be put to before being torn down. Houses all around it must have been torn down to make the large gravelled lot where the buses pulled in. There were still some trees at the edge of the lot and under them a few rows of chairs that she had not noticed when she got off the bus before noon. Two men were sitting on what used to be the veranda of the house, on old car seats. They wore brown shirts with the bus company's insignia but they seemed to be halfhearted about their work, not getting up when she asked if the bus to Carstairs was leaving at six o'clock as scheduled and where could she get a soft drink?

Six o'clock, far as they knew.

Coffee shop down the street.

Cooler inside but only Coke and orange left.

She got herself a Coca-Cola out of the cooler in a dirty little indoor waiting room that smelled of a bad toilet. Moving the depot to this dilapidated house must have thrown everyone into a state of indolence and fecklessness. There was a fan in the room they used as an office, and she saw, as she went by, some papers blow off the desk. "Oh, shit," said the office girl, and stamped her heel on them.

The chairs set up in the shade of the dusty city trees were straight-backed old wooden chairs originally painted different colors—they looked as if they had come from various kitchens. Strips of old carpet and rubber bathroom mats were laid down in front of them, to keep your feet off the gravel. Behind the first row of chairs she thought she saw a sheep lying on the ground, but it turned into a dirty-white dog, which trotted over and looked at her for a moment in a grave semi-official way—gave a brief sniff at her shoes, and trotted away. She had not noticed if there were any drinking straws and did not feel like going back to look. She drank Coke from the bottle, tilting back her head and closing her eyes.

When she opened them, a man was sitting one chair away, and was speaking to her.

"I got here as soon as I could," he said. "Nancy said you were going to catch a bus. As soon as I finished with the speech, I took off. But the bus depot is all torn up."

"Temporarily," she said.

"I knew you right away," he said. "In spite of—well, many years. When I saw you, I was talking to somebody. Then I looked again and you'd disappeared."

"I don't recognize you," said Louisa.

"Well, no," he said. "I guess not. Of course. You wouldn't."

He was wearing tan slacks, a pale-yellow short-sleeved shirt, a cream-and-yellow ascot scarf. A bit of a dandy, for a union man. His hair was white but thick and wavy, the sort of springy hair that goes in ripples, up and back from the forehead, his skin was flushed and his face was deeply wrinkled from the efforts of speechmaking—and from talking to people privately, she supposed, with much of the fervor and persuasiveness of his public speeches. He wore tinted glasses, which he took off now, as if willing that she should see him better. His eyes were a light blue, slightly bloodshot and apprehensive. A good-looking man, still trim except for a little authoritative bulge over the belt, but she did not find these serviceable good looks—the careful sporty clothes, the display of ripply hair, the effective expressions—very attractive. She preferred the kind of looks Arthur had. The restraint, the dark-suited dignity that some people could call pompous, that seemed to her admirable and innocent.

"I always meant to break the ice," he said. "I meant to speak to you. I should have gone in and said good-bye at least. The opportunity to leave came up so suddenly."

Louisa did not have any idea what to say to this. He sighed. He said, "You must have been mad at me. Are you still?"

"No," she said, and fell back, ridiculously, on the usual courtesies. "How is Grace? How is your daughter? Lillian?"

"Grace is not so well. She had some arthritis. Her weight doesn't help it. Lillian is all right. She's married but she still teaches high school. Mathematics. Not too usual for a woman."

How could Louisa begin to correct him? Could she say, No, your wife Grace got married again during the war, she married a farmer, a widower. Before that she used to come in and clean our house once a week. Mrs. Feare had got too old. And Lillian never finished high school, how could she be a high-school teacher? She married young, she had some children, she works in the drugstore. She had your height and your hair, dyed blond. I often looked at her and thought she must be like you. When she was growing up, I used to give her my stepdaughter's outgrown clothes.

Instead of this, she said, "Then the woman in the green dress—that was not Lillian?"

"Nancy? Oh, no! Nancy is my guardian angel. She keeps track of where I'm going, and when, and have I got my speech, and what I drink and eat and have I taken my pills. I tend toward high blood pressure. Nothing too serious. But my way of life's no good. I'm on the go constantly. Tonight I've got to fly out of here to Ottawa, tomorrow I've got a tough meeting, tomorrow night I've got some fool banquet."

Louisa felt it necessary to say, "You knew that I got married? I married Arthur Doud."

She thought he showed some surprise. But he said, "Yes, I heard that. Yes."

"We worked hard, too," said Louisa sturdily. "Arthur died six years ago. We kept the factory going all through the thirties even though at times we were down to three men. We had no money for repairs and I remember cutting up the office awnings so that Arthur could carry them up on a ladder and patch the roof. We tried making everything we could think of. Even outdoor bowling alleys for those amusement places. Then the war came and we couldn't keep up. We could sell all the pianos we could make but also we were making radar cases for the Navy. I stayed in the office all through."

"It must have been a change," he said, in what seemed a tactful voice. "A change from the Library."

"Work is work," she said. "I still work. My stepdaughter Bea is divorced, she keeps house for me after a fashion. My son has finally finished university—he is supposed to be learning about the business, but he has some excuse to go off in the middle of every afternoon. When I come home at suppertime, I am so tired I could drop, and I hear the ice tinkling in their glasses and them laughing behind the hedge. Oh, Mud, they say when they see me, Oh, poor Mud, sit down here, get her a drink!

They call me Mud because that was my son's name for me when he was a baby. But they are neither of them babies now. The house is cool when I come home—it's a lovely house if you remember, built in three tiers like a wedding cake. Mosaic tiles in the entrance hall. But I am always thinking about the factory, that is what fills my mind. What should we do to stay afloat? There are only five factories in Canada making pianos now, and three of them are in Quebec with the low cost of labor. No doubt you know all about that. When I talk to Arthur in my head, it is always about the same thing. I am very close to him still but it is hardly in a mystical way. You would think as you get older your mind would fill up with what they call the spiritual side of things, but mine just seems to get more and more practical, trying to get something settled. What a thing to talk to a dead man about."

She stopped, she was embarrassed. But she was not sure that he had listened to all of this, and in fact she was not sure that she had said all of it.

"What started me off—" he said. "What got me going in the first place, with whatever I have managed to do, was the Library. So I owe you a great deal."

He put his hands on his knees, let his head fall.

"Ah, rubbish," he said.

He groaned, and ended up with a laugh.

"My father," he said, "you wouldn't remember my father?"

"Oh, yes."

"Well. Sometimes I think he had the right idea."

Then he lifted his head, gave it a shake, and made a pronouncement.

"Love never dies."

She felt impatient to the point of taking offense. This is what all the speechmaking turns you into, she thought, a person who can say things like that. Love dies all the time, or at any rate it becomes distracted, overlaid—it might as well be dead.

"Arthur used to come and sit in the Library," she said. "In the beginning I was very provoked with him. I used to look at the back of his neck and think, Ha, what if something should hit you there! None of that would make sense to you. It wouldn't make sense. And it turned out to be something else I wanted entirely. I wanted to marry him and get into a normal life.

"A normal life," she repeated—and a giddiness seemed to be taking over, a widespread forgiveness of folly, alerting the skin of her spotty hand, her dry thick fingers that lay not far from his, on the seat of the chair between them. An amorous flare-up of the cells, of old intentions. *Oh, never dies.*

Across the gravelled yard came a group of oddly dressed folk. They moved all together, a clump of black. The women did not show their hair—they had black shawls or bonnets covering their heads. The men wore broad hats and black braces. The children were dressed just like their elders, even to the bonnets and hats. How hot they all looked in those clothes—how hot and dusty and wary and shy.

"The Tolpuddle Martyrs," he said, in a faintly joking, resigned, and compassionate voice. "Ah, I guess I'd better go over. I'd better go over there and have a word with them."

That edge of a joke, the uneasy kindness, made her think of somebody else. Who was it? When she saw the breadth of his shoulders from behind, and the broad flat buttocks, she knew who.

Jim Frarey.

Oh, what kind of a trick was being played on her, or what kind of trick was she playing on herself! She would not have it. She pulled herself up tightly, she saw all those black clothes melt into a puddle. She was dizzy and humiliated. She would not have it.

But not all black, now that they were getting closer. She could see dark blue, those were the men's shirts, and dark blue and purple in some of the women's dresses. She could see faces—the men's behind beards, the women's in their deep-brimmed bonnets. And now she knew who they were. They were Mennonites.

Mennonites were living in this part of the country, where they never used to be. There were some of them around Bondi, a village north of Carstairs. They would be going home on the same bus as she was.

He was not with them, or anywhere in sight.

A traitor, helplessly. A traveller.

Once she knew that they were Mennonites and not some lost unidentifiable strangers, these people did not look so shy or dejected. In fact they seemed quite cheerful, passing around a bag of candy, adults eating candy with the children. They settled on the chairs all around her.

No wonder she was feeling clammy. She had gone under a wave, which nobody else had noticed. You could say anything you liked about what had happened—but what it amounted to was going under a wave. She had gone under and through it and was left with a cold sheen on her skin, a beating in her ears, a cavity in her chest, and revolt in her stomach. It was anarchy she was up against—a devouring muddle. Sudden holes and impromptu tricks and radiant vanishing consolations.

But these Mennonite settlings are a blessing. The plop of behinds on chairs, the crackling of the candy bag, the meditative sucking and soft conversations. Without looking at Louisa, a little girl holds out the bag, and Louisa accepts a butterscotch mint. She is surprised to be able to hold it in her hand, to have her lips shape thank-you, then to discover in her mouth just the taste that she expected. She sucks on it as they do on theirs, not in any hurry, and allows that taste to promise her some reasonable continuance.

Lights have come on, though it isn't yet evening. In the trees above the wooden chairs someone has strung lines of little colored bulbs that she did not notice until now. They make her think of festivities. Carnivals. Boats of singers on the lake.

"What place is this?" she said to the woman beside her.

On the day of Miss Tamblyn's death it happened that Louisa was staying in the Commercial Hotel. She was a traveller then for a company that sold hats, ribbons, handkerchiefs and trimmings, and ladies' underwear to retail stores. She heard the talk in the hotel, and it occurred to her that the town would soon need a new Librarian. She was getting very tired of lugging her sample cases on and off trains, and showing her wares in hotels, packing and unpacking. She went at once and talked to the people in charge of the Library. A Mr. Doud and a Mr. Macleod. They sounded like a vaudeville team but did not look it. The pay was poor, but she had not been doing so well on commission, either. She told them that she had finished high school, in Toronto, and had worked in Eaton's Book Department before she switched to travelling. She did not think it necessary to tell them that she had only worked there five months when she was discovered to have t.b., and that she had then spent four years in a sanitorium. The t.b. was cured, anyway, her spots were dry.

The hotel moved her to one of the rooms for permanent guests, on the third floor. She could see the snow-covered hills over the rooftops. The town of Carstairs was in a river valley. It had three or four thousand people and a long main street that ran downhill, over the river, and uphill again. There was a piano and organ factory.

The houses were built for lifetimes and the yards were wide and the streets were lined with mature elm and maple trees. She had never been here when the leaves were on the trees. It must make a great difference. So much that lay open now would be concealed.

She was glad of a fresh start, her spirits were hushed and grateful. She had made fresh starts before and things had not turned out as she had hoped, but she believed in the swift decision, the unforeseen intervention, the uniqueness of her fate.

The town was full of the smell of horses. As evening came on, big blinkered horses with feathered hooves pulled the sleighs across the bridge, past the hotel, beyond the streetlights, down the dark side roads. Somewhere out in the country they would lose the sound of each other's bells.

HATESHIP, FRIENDSHIP, COURTSHIP, LOVESHIP, MARRIAGE

Years ago, before the trains stopped running on so many of the branch lines, a woman with a high, freckled forehead and a frizz of reddish hair came into the railway station and inquired about shipping furniture.

The station agent often tried a little teasing with women, especially the plain ones who seemed to appreciate it.

"Furniture?" he said, as if nobody had ever had such an idea before. "Well. Now. What kind of furniture are we talking about?"

A dining-room table and six chairs. A full bedroom suite, a sofa, a coffee table, end tables, a floor lamp. Also a china cabinet and a buffet.

"Whoa there. You mean a houseful."

"It shouldn't count as that much," she said. "There's no kitchen things and only enough for one bedroom."

Her teeth were crowded to the front of her mouth as if they were ready for an argument.

"You'll be needing the truck," he said.

"No. I want to send it on the train. It's going out west, to Saskatchewan."

She spoke to him in a loud voice as if he was deaf or stupid, and there was something wrong with the way she pronounced her words. An accent. He thought of Dutch—the Dutch were moving in around here—but she didn't have the heft of the Dutch women or the nice pink skin or the fair hair. She might have been under forty, but what did it matter? No beauty queen, ever.

He turned all business.

"First you'll need the truck to get it here from wherever you got it. And we better see if it's a place in Saskatchewan where the train goes through. Otherways you'd have to arrange to get it picked up, say, in Regina."

"It's Gdynia," she said. "The train goes through."

He took down a greasy-covered directory that was hanging from a nail and asked how she would spell that. She helped herself to the pencil that was also on a string and wrote on a piece of paper from her purse: *G D Y N I A.*

"What kind of nationality would that be?"

She said she didn't know.

He took back the pencil to follow from line to line.

"A lot of places out there it's all Czechs or Hungarians or Ukrainians," he said. It came to him as he said this that she might be one of those. But so what, he was only stating a fact.

"Here it is, all right, it's on the line."

"Yes," she said. "I want to ship it Friday—can you do that?"

"We can ship it, but I can't promise what day it'll get there," he said. "It all depends on the priorities. Somebody going to be on the lookout for it when it comes in?"

"Yes."

"It's a mixed train Friday, two-eighteen p.m. Truck picks it up Friday morning. You live here in town?"

She nodded, writing down the address. 106 Exhibition Road.

It was only recently that the houses in town had been numbered, and he couldn't picture the place, though he knew where Exhibition Road was. If she'd said the name McCauley at that time he might have taken more of an interest, and things might have turned out differently. There were new houses out there, built since the war, they were called "wartime houses." He supposed it must be one of those.

"Pay when you ship," he told her.

"Also, I want a ticket for myself on the same train. Friday afternoon."

"Going same place?"

"Yes."

"You can travel on the same train to Toronto, but then you have to wait for the Transcontinental, goes out ten-thirty at night. You want sleeper or coach? Sleeper you get a berth, coach you sit up in the day car."

She said she would sit up.

"Wait in Sudbury for the Montreal train, but you won't get off there, they'll just shunt you around and hitch on the Montreal cars. Then on to Port Arthur and then to Kenora. You don't get off till Regina, and there you have to get off and catch the branch-line train."

She nodded as if he should just get on and give her the ticket.

Slowing down, he said, "But I won't promise your furniture'll arrive when you do, I wouldn't think it would get in till a day or two after. It's all the priorities. Somebody coming to meet you?"

"Yes."

"Good. Because it won't likely be much of a station. Towns out there, they're not like here. They're mostly pretty rudimentary affairs."

She paid for the passenger ticket now, from a roll of bills in a cloth bag in her purse. Like an old lady. She counted her change, too. But not the way an old lady would count it—she held it in her hand and flicked her eyes over it, but you could tell she didn't miss a penny. Then she turned away rudely, without a good-bye.

"See you Friday," he called out.

She wore a long, drab coat on this warm September day, also a pair of clunky laced-up shoes, and ankle socks.

He was getting a coffee out of his thermos when she came back and rapped on the wicket.

"The furniture I'm sending," she said. "It's all good furniture, it's like new. I wouldn't want it to get scratched or banged up or in any way damaged. I don't want it to smell like livestock, either."

"Oh, well," he said. "The railway's pretty used to shipping things. And they don't use the same cars for shipping furniture they use for shipping pigs."

"I'm concerned that it gets there in just as good a shape as it leaves here."

"Well, you know, when you buy your furniture, it's in the store, right? But did you ever think how it got there? It wasn't made in the store, was it? No. It was made in some factory someplace, and it got shipped to the store, and that was done quite possibly by train. So that being the case, doesn't it stand to reason the railway knows how to look after it?"

She continued to look at him without a smile or any admission of her female foolishness.

"I hope so," she said. "I hope they do."

The station agent would have said, without thinking about it, that he knew everybody in town. Which meant that he knew about half of them. And most of those he knew were the core people, the ones who really were "in town" in the sense that they had not arrived yesterday and had no plans to move on.

He did not know the woman who was going to Saskatchewan because she did not go to his church or teach his children in school or work in any store or restaurant or office that he went into. Nor was she married to any of the men he knew in the Elks or the Oddfellows or the Lions Club or the Legion. A look at her left hand while she was getting the money out had told him—and he was not surprised—that she was not married to anybody. With those shoes, and ankle socks instead of stockings, and no hat or gloves in the afternoon, she might have been a farm woman. But she didn't have the hesitation they generally had, the embarrassment. She didn't have country manners—in fact, she had no manners at all. She had treated him as if he was an information machine. Besides, she had written a town address—Exhibition Road. The person she really reminded him of was a plainclothes nun he had seen on television, talking about the missionary work she did somewhere in the jungle—probably they had got out of their nuns' clothes there because it made it easier for them to clamber around. This nun had smiled once in a while to show that her religion was supposed to make people happy, but most of the time she looked out at her audience as if she believed that other people were mainly in the world for her to boss around.

One more thing Johanna meant to do she had been putting off doing. She had to go into the dress shop called Milady's and buy herself an outfit. She had never been inside that shop—when she had to buy anything, like socks, she went to Callaghans Mens Ladies and Childrens Wear. She had lots of clothes inherited from Mrs. Willets, things like this coat that would never wear out. And Sabitha—the girl she looked after, in Mr. McCauley's house—was showered with costly hand-me-downs from her cousins.

In Milady's window there were two mannequins wearing suits with quite short skirts and boxy jackets. One suit was a rusty-gold color and the other a soft deep green. Big gaudy paper maple leaves were scattered round the mannequins' feet and pasted here and there on the window. At the time of year when most people's concern was to rake up leaves and burn them, here they were the chosen thing. A sign written in flowing black script was stuck diagonally across the glass. It said: *Simple Elegance, the Mode for Fall.*

She opened the door and went inside.

Right ahead of her, a full-length mirror showed her in Mrs. Willets's high-quality but shapeless long coat, with a few inches of lumpy bare legs above the ankle socks.

They did that on purpose, of course. They set the mirror there so you could get a proper notion of your deficiencies, right away, and then—they hoped—you would jump to the conclusion that you had to buy something to alter the picture. Such a transparent trick that it would have made her walk out, if she had not come in determined, knowing what she had to get.

Along one wall was a rack of evening dresses, all fit for belles of the ball with their net and taffeta, their dreamy colors. And beyond them, in a glass case so no profane fingers could get at them, half a dozen wedding gowns, pure white froth or vanilla satin or ivory lace, embroidered in silver beads or seed pearls. Tiny bodices, scalloped necklines, lavish skirts. Even when she was younger she could never have contemplated such extravagance, not just in the matter of money but in expectations, in the preposterous hope of transformation, and bliss.

It was two or three minutes before anybody came. Maybe they had a peephole and were eyeing her, thinking she wasn't their kind of customer and hoping she would go away.

She would not. She moved beyond the mirror's reflection—

stepping from the linoleum by the door to a plushy rug—and at long last the curtain at the back of the store opened and out stepped Milady herself, dressed in a black suit with glittery buttons. High heels, thin ankles, girdle so tight her nylons rasped, gold hair skinned back from her made-up face.

"I thought I could try on the suit in the window," Johanna said in a rehearsed voice. "The green one."

"Oh, that's a lovely suit," the woman said. "The one in the window happens to be a size ten. Now you look to be—maybe a fourteen?"

She rasped ahead of Johanna back to the part of the store where the ordinary clothes, the suits and daytime dresses, were hung.

"You're in luck. Fourteen coming up."

The first thing Johanna did was look at the price tag. Easily twice what she'd expected, and she was not going to pretend otherwise.

"It's expensive enough."

"It's very fine wool." The woman monkeyed around till she found the label, then read off a description of the material that Johanna wasn't really listening to because she had caught at the hem to examine the workmanship.

"It feels as light as silk, but it wears like iron. You can see it's lined throughout, lovely silk-and-rayon lining. You won't find it bagging in the seat and going out of shape the way the cheap suits do. Look at the velvet cuffs and collar and the little velvet buttons on the sleeve."

"I see them."

"That's the kind of detail you pay for, you just do not get it otherwise. I love the velvet touch. It's only on the green one, you know—the apricot one doesn't have it, even though they're exactly the same price."

Indeed it was the velvet collar and cuffs that gave the suit, in Johanna's eyes, its subtle look of luxury and made her long to buy it. But she was not going to say so.

"I might as well go ahead and try it on."

This was what she'd come prepared for, after all. Clean underwear and fresh talcum powder under her arms.

The woman had enough sense to leave her alone in the bright cubicle. Johanna avoided the glass like poison till she'd got the skirt straight and the jacket done up.

At first she just looked at the suit. It was all right. The fit was all right—the skirt shorter than what she was used to, but then what she was used to was not the style. There was no problem with the suit. The problem was with what stuck out of it. Her neck and her face and her hair and her big hands and thick legs.

"How are you getting on? Mind if I take a peek?"

Peek all you want to, Johanna thought, it's a case of a sow's ear, as you'll soon see.

The woman tried looking from one side, then the other.

"Of course, you'll need your nylons on and your heels. How does it feel? Comfortable?"

"The suit feels fine," Johanna said. "There's nothing the matter with the suit."

The woman's face changed in the mirror. She stopped smiling. She looked disappointed and tired, but kinder.

"Sometimes that's just the way it is. You never really know until you try something on. The thing is," she said, with a new, more moderate conviction growing in her voice, "the thing is you have a fine figure, but it's a strong figure. You have large bones and what's the matter with that? Dinky little velvet-covered buttons are not for you. Don't bother with it anymore. Just take it off."

Then when Johanna had got down to her underwear there was a tap and a hand through the curtain.

"Just slip this on, for the heck of it."

A brown wool dress, lined, with a full skirt gracefully gathered, three-quarter sleeves and a plain round neckline. About as plain as you could get, except for a narrow gold belt. Not as expensive as the suit, but still the price seemed like a lot, when you considered all there was to it.

At least the skirt was a more decent length and the fabric made a noble swirl around her legs. She steeled herself and looked in the glass.

This time she didn't look as if she'd been stuck into the garment for a joke.

The woman came and stood beside her, and laughed, but with relief.

"It's the color of your eyes. You don't need to wear velvet. You've got velvet eyes."

That was the kind of soft-soaping Johanna would have felt bound to scoff at, except that at the moment it seemed to be true. Her eyes were not large, and if asked to describe their color she would have said, "I guess they're a kind of brown." But now they looked to be a really deep brown, soft and shining.

It wasn't that she had suddenly started thinking she was pretty or anything. Just that her eyes were a nice color, if they had been a piece of cloth.

"Now, I bet you don't wear dress shoes very often," the woman said. "But if you had nylons on and just a minimum kind of pump—And I bet you don't wear jewelry, and you're quite right, you don't need to, with that belt."

To cut off the sales spiel Johanna said, "Well, I better take it off so you can wrap it up." She was sorry to lose the soft weight of the skirt and the discreet ribbon of gold around her waist.

She had never in her life had this silly feeling of being enhanced by what she had put on herself.

"I just hope it's for a special occasion," the woman called out as Johanna was hastening into her now dingy-looking regular clothes.

"It'll likely be what I get married in," said Johanna.

She was surprised at that coming out of her mouth. It wasn't a major error—the woman didn't know who she was and would probably not be talking to anybody who did know. Still, she had meant to keep absolutely quiet. She must have felt she owed this person something—that they'd been through the disaster of the green suit and the discovery of the brown dress together and that was a bond. Which was nonsense. The woman was in the business of selling clothes, and she'd just succeeded in doing that.

"Oh!" the woman cried out. "Oh, that's wonderful."

Well, it might be, Johanna thought, and then again it might not. She might be marrying anybody. Some miserable farmer who wanted a workhorse around the place, or some wheezy old half-cripple looking for a nurse. This woman had no idea what kind of man she had lined up, and it wasn't any of her business anyway.

"I can tell it's a love match," the woman said, just as if she had read these disgruntled thoughts. "That's why your eyes were shining in the mirror. I've wrapped it all in tissue paper, all you have to do is take it out and hang it up and the material will fall out beautifully. Just give it a light press if you want, but you probably won't even need to do that."

Then there was the business of handing over the money. They both pretended not to look, but both did.

"It's worth it," the woman said. "You only get married the once. Well, that's not always strictly true—"

"In my case it'll be true," Johanna said. Her face was hotly flushed because marriage had not, in fact, been mentioned. Not even in the last letter. She had revealed to this woman what she was counting on, and that had perhaps been an unlucky thing to do.

"Where did you meet him?" said the woman, still in that tone of wistful gaiety. "What was your first date?"

"Through family," Johanna said truthfully. She wasn't meaning to say any more but heard herself go on. "The Western Fair. In London."

"The Western Fair," the woman said. "In London." She could have been saying "the Castle Ball."

"We had his daughter and her friend with us," said Johanna, thinking that in a way it would have been more accurate to say that he and Sabitha and Edith had her, Johanna, with them.

"Well, I can say my day has not been wasted. I've provided the dress for somebody to be a happy bride in. That's enough to justify my existence." The woman tied a narrow pink ribbon around the dress box, making a big, unnecessary bow, then gave it a wicked snip with the scissors.

"I'm here all day," she said. "And sometimes I just wonder what I think I'm doing. I ask myself, What do you think you're doing here? I put up a new display in the window and I do this and that to entice the people in, but there are days—there are *days*—when I do not see one soul come in that door. I know— people think these clothes are too expensive—but they're *good*. They're good clothes. If you want the quality you have to pay the price."

"They must come in when they want something like those," said Johanna, looking toward the evening dresses. "Where else could they go?"

"That's just it. They don't. They go to the city—that's where they go. They'll drive fifty miles, a hundred miles, never mind the gas, and tell themselves that way they get something better than I've got here. And they haven't. Not better quality, not better selection. Nothing. Just that they'd be ashamed to say they bought their wedding outfits in town. Or they'll come in and try something on and say they have to think about it. I'll be back, they say. And I think, Oh, yes, I know what that means. It means they'll try to find the same thing cheaper in London or Kitchener, and even if it isn't cheaper, they'll buy it there once they've driven all that way and got sick of looking.

"I don't know," she said. "Maybe if I was a local person it would make a difference. It's very clique-y here, I find. You're not local, are you?"

Johanna said, "No."

"Don't you find it clique-y?"

Cleeky.

."Hard for an outsider to break in, is what I mean."

"I'm used to being on my own," Johanna said.

"But you found somebody. You won't be on your own anymore and isn't that lovely? Some days I think how grand it would be, to be married and stay at home. Of course, I used to be married, and I worked anyway. Ah, well. Maybe the man in the moon will walk in here and fall in love with me and then I'll be all set!"

Johanna had to hurry—that woman's need for conversation had delayed her. She was hurrying to be back at the house, her purchase stowed away, before Sabitha got home from school.

Then she remembered that Sabitha wasn't there, having been carried off on the weekend by her mother's cousin, her Aunt Roxanne, to live like a proper rich girl in Toronto and go to a rich girl's school. But she continued to walk fast—so fast some smart aleck holding up the wall of the drugstore called out to her, "Where's the fire?" and she slowed down a bit, not to attract attention.

The dress box was awkward—how could she have known the store would have its own pink cardboard boxes, with *Milady's* written across them in purple handwriting? A dead giveaway.

She felt a fool for mentioning a wedding, when he hadn't mentioned it and she ought to remember that. So much else had been said—or written—such fondness and yearning expressed, that the actual marrying seemed just to have been overlooked. The way you might speak about getting up in the morning and not about having breakfast, though you certainly intended to have it.

Nevertheless she should have kept her mouth shut.

She saw Mr. McCauley walking in the opposite direction up the other side of the street. That was all right—even if he had met her head-on he would never have noticed the box she carried. He would have raised a finger to his hat and passed her by, presumably noticing that she was his housekeeper but possibly not. He had other things on his mind, and for all anybody knew might be looking at some town other than the one they saw. Every working day—and sometimes, forgetfully, on holidays or Sundays—he got dressed in one of his three-piece suits and his light overcoat or his heavy overcoat, and his gray fedora and his well-polished shoes, and walked from Exhibition Road uptown to the office he still maintained over what had been the harness and luggage store. It was spoken of as an Insurance Office, though it was quite a long time since he had actively sold insurance. Sometimes people climbed the stairs to see him, maybe to ask some question about their policies or more likely about lot boundaries, the history of some piece of real estate in town or farm out in the country. His office was full of maps old and new, and he liked nothing better than to lay them out and get into a discussion that expanded far beyond the question asked. Three or four times a day he emerged and walked the street, as now. During the war he had put the McLaughlin-Buick up on blocks in the barn, and walked everywhere to set an example. He still seemed to be setting an example, fifteen years later. Hands clasped behind his back, he was like a kind landlord inspecting his property or a preacher happy to observe his flock. Of course, half the people that he met had no idea who he was.

The town had changed, even in the time Johanna had been here. Trade was moving out to the highway, where there was a new discount store and a Canadian Tire and a motel with a lounge and topless dancers. Some downtown shops had tried to spruce themselves up with pink or mauve or olive paint, but already that paint was curling on the old brick and some of the interiors were empty. Milady's was almost certain to follow suit.

If Johanna was the woman in there, what would she have done? She'd never have gotten in so many elaborate evening dresses, for a start. What instead? If you made the switch to cheaper clothes you'd only be putting yourself in competition with Callaghans and the discount place, and there probably wasn't trade enough to go around. So what about going into fancy baby clothes, children's clothes, trying to pull in the grandmothers and aunts who had the money and would spend it for that kind of thing? Forget about the mothers, who would go to Callaghans, having less money and more sense.

But if it was her in charge—Johanna—she would never be able to pull in anybody. She could see what needed to be done, and how, and she could round up and supervise people to do it, but she could never charm or entice. Take it or leave it, would be her attitude. No doubt they would leave it.

It was the rare person who took to her, and she'd been aware of that for a long time. Sabitha certainly hadn't shed any tears when she said good-bye—though you could say Johanna was the nearest thing Sabitha had to a mother, since her own mother had died. Mr. McCauley would be upset when she left because she'd given good service and it would be hard to replace her, but that would be all he thought about. Both he and his grand-daughter were spoiled and self-centered. As for the neighbors, they would no doubt rejoice. Johanna had had problems on both sides of the property. On one side it was the neighbors' dog digging in her garden, burying and retrieving his supply of bones, which he could better have done at home. And on the other it was the black cherry tree, which was on the McCauleys' property but bore most of its cherries on the branches hanging over into the next yard. In both cases she had raised a fuss, and won. The dog was tied up and the other neighbors left the cherries alone. If she got up on the stepladder she could reach well over into their yard, but they no longer chased the birds out of the branches and it made a difference to the crop.

Mr. McCauley would have let them pick. He would have let the dog dig. He would let himself be taken advantage of. Part of the reason was that these were new people and lived in new houses and so he preferred not to pay attention to them. At one time there had been just three or four large houses on Exhibition Road. Across from them were the fairgrounds, where the fall fair was held (officially called the Agricultural Exhibition, hence the name), and in between were orchard trees, small meadows. A dozen years ago or so that land had been sold off in regular lot sizes and houses had been put up—small houses in alternating styles, one kind with an upstairs and the other kind without. Some were already getting to look pretty shabby.

There were only a couple of houses whose occupants Mr. McCauley knew and was friendly with—the schoolteacher, Miss Hood, and her mother, and the Shultzes, who ran the Shoe Repair shop. The Shultzes' daughter, Edith, was or had been Sabitha's great friend. It was natural, with their being in the same grade at school—at least last year, once Sabitha had been held back—and living near each other. Mr. McCauley hadn't minded—maybe he had some idea that Sabitha would be removed before long to live a different sort of life in Toronto. Johanna would not have chosen Edith, though the girl was never rude, never troublesome when she came to the house. And she was not stupid. That might have been the problem— she was smart and Sabitha was not so smart. She had made Sabitha sly.

That was all over now. Now that the cousin, Roxanne—Mrs. Huber—had shown up, the Schultz girl was all part of Sabitha's childish past.

> *I am going to arrange to get all your furniture out to you on the train as soon as they can take it and prepaid as soon as they tell me what it will cost. I have been thinking you will need it now. I guess it will not be that much of a surprise that I thought you would not mind if I went along to be of help to you as I hope I can be.*

This was the letter she had taken to the Post Office, before she went to make arrangements at the railway station. It was the first letter she had ever sent to him directly. The others had been slipped in with the letters she made Sabitha write. And his to her had come in the same way, tidily folded and with her name, Johanna, typed on the back of the page so there would be no mistaking. That kept the people in the Post Office from catching on, and it never hurt to save a stamp. Of course, Sabitha could have reported to her grandfather, or even read what was written to Johanna, but Sabitha was no more interested in communicating with the old man than she was in letters—the writing or the receiving of them.

The furniture was stored back in the barn, which was just a town barn, not a real barn with animals and a granary. When Johanna got her first look at everything a year or so ago, she found it grimy with dust and splattered with pigeon droppings. The pieces had been piled in carelessly without anything to cover them. She had hauled what she could carry out into the yard, leaving space in the barn to get at the big pieces she couldn't carry—the sofa and buffet and china cabinet and dining table. The bedstead she could take apart. She went at the wood with soft dustrags, then lemon oil, and when she finished it shone like candy. Maple candy—it was bird's-eye maple wood. It looked glamorous to her, like satin bedspreads and blond hair. Glamorous and modern, a total contrast to all the dark wood and irksome carving of the furniture she cared for in the house. She thought of it as *his* furniture then, and still did when she got it out this Wednesday. She had put old quilts over the bottom layer to protect everything there from what was piled on top, and sheets over what was on top to protect that from the birds, and as a result there was only a light dust. But she wiped everything and lemon-oiled it before she put it back, protected in the same way, to wait for the truck on Friday.

Dear Mr. McCauley,

I am leaving on the train this afternoon (Friday). I realize this is without giving my notice to you, but I will waive my last pay, which would be three weeks owing this coming Monday. There is a beef stew on the stove in the double boiler that just needs warming up. Enough there for three meals or maybe could be stretched to a fourth. As soon as it is hot and you have got all you want, put the lid on and put it away in the fridge. Remember, put the lid on at once not to take chances with it getting spoiled. Regards to you and to Sabitha and will probably be in touch when I am settled. Johanna Parry.

P.S. I have shipped his furniture to Mr. Boudreau as he may need it. Remember to make sure when you reheat there is enough water in bottom part of the double boiler.

Mr. McCauley had no trouble finding out that the ticket Johanna had bought was to Gdynia, Saskatchewan. He phoned the station agent and asked. He could not think how to describe Johanna—was she old or young-looking, thin or moderately heavy, what was the color of her coat?—but that was not necessary when he mentioned the furniture.

When this call came through there were a couple of people in the station waiting for the evening train. The agent tried to keep his voice down at first, but he became excited when he heard about the stolen furniture (what Mr. McCauley actually said was "and I believe she took some furniture with her"). He swore that if he had known who she was and what she was up to he would never have let her set foot on the train. This assertion was heard and repeated and believed, nobody asking how he could have stopped a grown woman who had paid for her ticket, unless he had some proof right away that she was a thief. Most people who repeated his words believed that he could and would have stopped her—they believed in the authority of station agents and of upright-walking fine old men in three-piece suits like Mr. McCauley.

The beef stew was excellent, as Johanna's cooking always was, but Mr. McCauley found he could not swallow it. He disregarded the instruction about the lid and left the pot sitting open on the stove and did not even turn off the burner until the water in the bottom pot boiled away and he was alerted by a smell of smoking metal.

This was the smell of treachery.

He told himself to be thankful at least that Sabitha was taken care of and he did not have that to worry about. His niece—

his wife's cousin, actually, Roxanne—had written to tell him that from what she had seen of Sabitha on her summer visit to Lake Simcoe the girl was going to take some handling.

"Frankly I don't think you and that woman you've hired are going to be up to it when the boys come swarming around."

She did not go so far as to ask him whether he wanted another Marcelle on his hands, but that was what she meant. She said she would get Sabitha into a good school where she could be taught manners at least.

He turned on the television for a distraction, but it was no use.

It was the furniture that galled him. It was Ken Boudreau.

The fact was that three days before—on the very day that Johanna had bought her ticket, as the station agent had now told him—Mr. McCauley had received a letter from Ken Boudreau asking him to (a) advance some money against the furniture belonging to him (Ken Boudreau) and his dead wife, Marcelle, which was stored in Mr. McCauley's barn, or (b) if he could not see his way to doing that, to sell the furniture for as much as he could get and send the money as quickly as he could to Saskatchewan. There was no mention of the loans that had already been made by father-in-law to son-in-law, all against the value of this furniture and amounting to more than it could ever be sold for. Could Ken Boudreau have forgotten all about that? Or did he simply hope—and this was more probable—that his father-in-law would have forgotten?

He was now, it seemed, the owner of a hotel. But his letter was full of diatribes against the fellow who had formerly owned it and who had misled him as to various particulars.

"If I can just get over this hurdle," he said, "then I am convinced I can still make a go of it." But what was the hurdle? A need for immediate money, but he did not say whether it was owing to the former owner, or to the bank, or to a private mortgage holder, or what. It was the same old story—a desperate, wheedling tone mixed in with some arrogance, some sense of its being what was owed him, because of the wounds inflicted on him, the shame suffered, on account of Marcelle.

With many misgivings but remembering that Ken Boudreau was after all his son-in-law and had fought in the war and been through God-knows-what trouble in his marriage, Mr. McCauley had sat down and written a letter saying that he did not have any idea how to go about getting the best price for the furniture and it would be very difficult for him to find out and that he was enclosing a check, which he would count as an outright personal loan. He wished his son-in-law to acknowledge it as such and to remember the number of similar loans made in the past—already, he believed, exceeding any value of the furniture. He was enclosing a list of dates and amounts. Apart from fifty dollars paid nearly two years ago (with a promise of regular payments to follow), he had received nothing. His son-in-law must surely understand that as a result of these unpaid and interest-free loans Mr. McCauley's income had declined, since he would otherwise have invested the money.

He had thought of adding, "I am not such a fool as you seem to think," but decided not to, since that would reveal his irritation and perhaps his weakness.

And now look. The man had jumped the gun and enlisted Johanna in his scheme—he would always be able to get around women—and got hold of the furniture as well as the check. She had paid for the shipping herself, the station agent had said. The flashy-looking modern maple stuff had been overvalued in the deals already made and they would not get much for it, especially when you counted what the railway had charged. If they had been cleverer they would simply have taken something from the house, one of the old cabinets or parlor settees too uncomfortable to sit on, made and bought in the last century. That, of course, would have been plain stealing. But what they had done was not far off.

He went to bed with his mind made up to prosecute.

He woke in the house alone, with no smell of coffee or breakfast coming from the kitchen—instead, there was a whiff of the burned pot still in the air. An autumn chill had settled in all the high-ceilinged, forlorn rooms. It had been warm last evening and on preceding evenings—the furnace had not been turned on yet, and when Mr. McCauley did turn it on the warm air was accompanied by a blast of cellar damp, of mold and earth and decay. He washed and dressed slowly, with forgetful pauses, and spread some peanut butter on a piece of bread for his breakfast. He belonged to a generation in which there were men who were said not to be able even to boil water, and he was one of them. He looked out the front windows and saw the trees on the other side of the racetrack swallowed up in the morning fog, which seemed to be advancing, not retreating as it should at this hour, across the track itself. He seemed to see in the fog the looming buildings of the old Exhibition Grounds—homely, spacious buildings, like enormous barns. They had stood for years and years unused—all through the war—and he forgot what happened to them in the end. Were they torn down, or did they fall down? He abhorred the races that took place now, the crowds and the loudspeaker and the illegal drinking and the ruinous uproar of the summer Sundays. When he thought of that he thought of his poor girl Marcelle, sitting on the verandah steps and calling out to grown schoolmates who had got out of their parked cars and were hurrying to see the races. The fuss she made, the joy she expressed at being back in town, the hugging and holding people up, talking a mile a minute, rattling on about childhood days and how she'd missed everybody. She had said that the only thing not perfect about life was missing her husband, Ken, left out west because of his work.

She went out there in her silk pajamas, with straggly, uncombed, dyed-blond hair. Her arms and legs were thin, but her face was somewhat bloated, and what she claimed was her tan seemed a sickly brown color not from the sun. Maybe jaundice.

The child had stayed inside and watched television—Sunday cartoons that she was surely too old for.

He couldn't tell what was wrong, or be sure that anything was. Marcelle went away to London to have some female thing done and died in the hospital. When he phoned her husband to tell him, Ken Boudreau said, "What did she take?"

If Marcelle's mother had been alive still, would things have been any different? The fact was that her mother, when she was alive, had been as bewildered as he was. She had sat in the kitchen crying while their teenage daughter, locked into her room, had climbed out the window and slid down the veran-dah roof to be welcomed by carloads of boys.

The house was full of a feeling of callous desertion, of deceit. He and his wife had surely been kind parents, driven to the wall by Marcelle. When she had eloped with an airman, they had hoped that she would be all right, at last. They had been generous to the two of them as to the most proper young couple. But it all fell apart. To Johanna Parry he had likewise been generous, and look how she too had gone against him.

He walked to town and went into the hotel for his breakfast. The waitress said, "You're bright and early this morning."

And while she was still pouring out his coffee he began to tell her about how his housekeeper had walked out on him without any warning or provocation, not only left her job with no notice but taken a load of furniture that had belonged to his daughter, that now was supposed to belong to his son-in-law but didn't really, having been bought with his daughter's wedding money. He told her how his daughter had married an airman, a good-looking, plausible fellow who wasn't to be trusted around the corner.

"Excuse me," the waitress said. "I'd love to chat, but I got people waiting on their breakfast. Excuse me—"

He climbed the stairs to his office, and there, spread out on his desk, were the old maps he had been studying yesterday in an effort to locate exactly the very first burying ground in the country (abandoned, he believed, in 1839). He turned on the light and sat down, but he found he could not concentrate. After the waitress's reproof—or what he took for a reproof—he hadn't been able to eat his breakfast or enjoy his coffee. He decided to go out for a walk to calm himself down.

But instead of walking along in his usual way, greeting people and passing a few words with them, he found himself bursting into speech. The minute anybody asked him how he was this morning he began in a most uncharacteristic, even shameful way to blurt out his woes, and like the waitress, these people had business to attend to and they nodded and shuffled and made excuses to get away. The morning didn't seem to be warming up in the way foggy fall mornings usually did; his jacket wasn't warm enough, so he sought the comfort of the shops.

People who had known him the longest were the most dismayed. He had never been anything but reticent—the well-mannered gentleman, his mind on other times, his courtesy a deft apology for privilege (which was a bit of a joke, because the privilege was mostly in his recollections and not apparent to others). He should have been the last person to air wrongs or ask for sympathy—he hadn't when his wife died, or even when his daughter died—yet here he was, pulling out some letter, asking if it wasn't a shame the way this fellow had taken him for money over and over again, and even now when he'd taken pity on him once more the fellow had connived with his housekeeper to steal the furniture. Some thought it was his own furniture he was talking about—they believed the old man had been left without a bed or a chair in his house. They advised him to go to the police.

"That's no good, that's no good," he said. "How can you get blood from a stone?"

He went into the Shoe Repair shop and greeted Herman Shultz.

"Do you remember those boots you resoled for me, the ones I got in England? You resoled them four or five years ago?"

The shop was like a cave, with shaded bulbs hanging down over various workplaces. It was abominably ventilated, but its manly smells—of glue and leather and shoe-blacking and fresh-cut felt soles and rotted old ones—were comfortable to Mr. McCauley. Here his neighbor Herman Shultz, a sallow, expert, spectacled workman, bent-shouldered, was occupied in all seasons—driving in iron nails and clinch nails and, with a wicked hooked knife, cutting the desired shapes out of leather. The felt was cut by something like a miniature circular saw. The buffers made a scuffing noise and the sandpaper wheel made a rasp and the emery stone on a tool's edge sang high like a mechanical insect and the sewing machine punched the leather in an earnest industrial rhythm. All the sounds and smells and precise activities of the place had been familiar to Mr. McCauley for years but never identified or reflected upon before. Now Herman, in his blackened leather apron with a boot on one hand, straightened up, smiled, nodded, and Mr. McCauley saw the man's whole life in this cave. He wished to express sympathy or admiration or something more that he didn't understand.

"Yes, I do," Herman said. "They were nice boots."

"Fine boots. You know I got them on my wedding trip. I got them in England. I can't remember now where, but it wasn't in London."

"I remember you telling me."

"You did a fine job on them. They're still doing well. Fine job, Herman. You do a good job here. You do honest work."

"That's good." Herman took a quick look at the boot on his hand. Mr. McCauley knew that the man wanted to get back to his work, but he couldn't let him.

"I've just had an eye-opener. A shock."

"Have you?"

The old man pulled out the letter and began to read bits of it aloud, with interjections of dismal laughter.

"Bronchitis. He says he's sick with bronchitis. He doesn't know where to turn. *I don't know who to turn to.* Well he always knows who to turn to. When he's run through everything else, turn to me. *A few hundred just till I get on my feet.* Begging and pleading with me and all the time he's conniving with my housekeeper. Did you know that? She stole a load of furniture and went off out west with it. They were hand in glove. This is a man I've saved the skin of, time and time again. And never a penny back. No, no, I have to be honest and say fifty dollars. Fifty out of hundreds and hundreds. Thousands. He was in the Air Force in the war, you know. Those shortish fellows, they were often in the Air Force. Strutting around thinking they were war heroes. Well, I guess I shouldn't say that, but I think the war spoiled some of those fellows, they never could adjust to life afterwards. But that's not enough of an excuse. Is it? I can't excuse him forever because of the war."

"No you can't."

"I knew he wasn't to be trusted the first time I met him. That's the extraordinary thing. I knew it and I let him rook me all the same. There are people like that. You take pity on them just for being the crooks they are. I got him his insurance job out there, I had some connections. Of course he mucked it up. A bad egg. Some just are."

"You're right about that."

Mrs. Shultz was not in the store that day. Usually she was the one at the counter, taking in the shoes and showing them to her husband and reporting back what he said, making out the slips, and taking the payment when the restored shoes were handed back. Mr. McCauley remembered that she had had some kind of operation during the summer.

"Your wife isn't in today? Is she well?"

"She thought she'd better take it easy today. I've got my girl in."

Herman Shultz nodded toward the shelves to the right of the counter, where the finished shoes were displayed. Mr. McCauley turned his head and saw Edith, the daughter, whom he hadn't noticed when he came in. A childishly thin girl with straight black hair, who kept her back to him, rearranging the shoes. That was just the way she had seemed to slide in and out of sight when she came to his house as Sabitha's friend. You never got a good look at her face.

"You're going to help you father out now?" Mr. McCauley said. "You're through with school?"

"It's Saturday," said Edith, half turning, faintly smiling.

"So it is. Well, it's a good thing to help your father, anyway. You must take care of your parents. They've worked hard and they're good people." With a slight air of apology, as if he knew he was being sententious, Mr. McCauley said, "Honor thy father and thy mother, that thy days may be long in the—"

Edith said something not for him to hear. She said, "Shoe Repair shop."

"I'm taking up your time, I'm imposing on you," said Mr. McCauley sadly. "You have work to do."

"There's no need for you to be sarcastic," said Edith's father when the old man had gone.

He told Edith's mother all about Mr. McCauley at supper.

"He's not himself," he said. "Something's come over him."

"Maybe a little stroke," she said. Since her own operation—for gallstones—she spoke knowledgeably and with a placid satisfaction about the afflictions of other people.

Now that Sabitha had gone, vanished into another sort of life that had, it seemed, always been waiting for her, Edith had reverted to being the person she had been before Sabitha came here. "Old for her age," diligent, critical. After three weeks at high school she knew she was going to be very good at all the new subjects—Latin, Algebra, English Literature. She believed that her cleverness was going to be recognized and acclaimed and an important future would open out for her. The past year's silliness with Sabitha was slipping out of sight.

Yet when she thought about Johanna's going off out west she felt a chill from her past, an invasive alarm. She tried to bang a lid down on that, but it wouldn't stay.

As soon as she had finished washing the dishes she went off to her room with the book they had been assigned for literature class. *David Copperfield.*

She was a child who had never received more than tepid reproofs from her parents—old parents to have a child of her age, which was said to account for her being the way she was—but she felt in perfect accord with David in his unhappy situation. She felt that she was one like him, one who might as well have been an orphan, because she would probably have to run away, go into hiding, fend for herself, when the truth became known and her past shut off her future.

It had all begun with Sabitha saying, on the way to school, "We have to go by the Post Office. I have to send a letter to my dad."

They walked to and from school together every day. Sometimes they walked with their eyes closed, or backwards. Sometimes when they met people they gabbled away softly in a nonsense language, to cause confusion. Most of their good ideas were Edith's. The only idea Sabitha introduced was the writing down of a boy's name and your own, and the stroking out of all letters that were duplicated and the counting of the remainder. Then you ticked off the counted number on your fingers, saying, *Hateship, friendship, courtship, loveship, marriage,* till you got the verdict on what could happen between you and that boy.

"That's a fat letter," said Edith. She noticed everything, and she remembered everything, quickly memorizing whole pages of the textbooks in a way the other children found sinister. "Did you have a lot of things to write to your dad?" she said, surprised, because she could not credit this—or at least could not credit that Sabitha would get them on paper.

"I only wrote on one page," Sabitha said, feeling the letter.

"A-ha," said Edith. "Ah. Ha."

"Aha what?"

"I bet she put something else in. Johanna did."

The upshot of this was that they did not take the letter directly to the Post Office, but saved it and steamed it open at Edith's house after school. They could do such things at Edith's house because her mother worked all day at the Shoe Repair shop.

Dear Mr. Ken Boudreau,

I just thought I would write and send my thanks to you for the nice things you said about me in your letter to your daughter. You do not need to worry about me leaving. You say that I am a person you can trust. That is the meaning I take and as far as I know it is true. I am grateful to you for saying that, since some people feel that a person like me that they do not know the background of is Beyond the Pale. So I thought I would tell you something about myself. I was born in Glasgow, but my mother had to give me up when she got married. I was taken to the Home at the age of five. I looked for her to come back, but she didn't and I got used to it there and they weren't Bad. At the age of eleven I was brought to Canada on a Plan and lived with the Dixons, working on their Market Gardens. School was in the Plan, but I didn't see much of it. In winter I worked in the house for the Mrs. but circumstances made me think of leaving, and being big and strong for my age got taken on at a Nursing Home looking after the old people. I did not mind the work, but for better money went and worked in a Broom Factory. Mr. Willets that owned it had an old mother that came in to see how things were going, and she and I took to each other some way. The atmosphere was giving me breathing troubles so she said I should come and work for her and I did. I lived with her 12 yrs. on a lake called Mourning Dove Lake up north. There was only the two of us, but I could take care of everything outside and in, even running the motorboat and driving the car. I learned to read properly because her eyes were going bad and she liked me to read to her. She died at the age of 96. You might say what a life for a young person, but I was happy. We ate together every meal and I slept in her room the last year and a half. But after she died the family gave me one

*wk. to pack up. She had left me some money and I guess they did
not like that. She wanted me to use it for Education but I would
have to go in with kids. So when I saw the ad Mr. McCauley put in
the Globe and Mail I came to see about it. I needed work to get over
missing Mrs. Willets. So I guess I have bored you long enough with
my History and you'll be relieved I have got up to the Present.
Thank you for your good opinion and for taking me along to the
Fair. I am not one for the rides or for eating the stuff but it was still
certainly a pleasure to be included.*

Your friend, Johanna Parry.

Edith read Johanna's words aloud, in an imploring voice and
with a woebegone expression.

"I was born in Glasgow, but my mother had to give me up
when she took one look at me—"

"Stop," said Sabitha. "I'm laughing so hard I'll be sick."

"How did she get her letter in with yours without you
knowing?"

"She just takes it from me and puts it in an envelope and
writes on the outside because she doesn't think my writing is
good enough."

Edith had to put Scotch tape on the flap of the envelope to
make it stick, since there wasn't enough sticky stuff left. "She's
in love with him," she said.

"Oh, puke-puke," said Sabitha, holding her stomach. "She
can't be. Old Johanna."

"What did he say about her, anyway?"

"Just about how I was supposed to respect her and it would
be too bad if she left because we were lucky to have her and he
didn't have a home for me and Grandpa couldn't raise a girl by
himself and blah-blah. He said she was a lady. He said he could
tell."

"So then she falls in lo-ove."

The letter remained with Edith overnight, lest Johanna discover that it hadn't been posted and was sealed with Scotch tape. They took it to the Post Office the next morning.

"Now we'll see what he writes back. Watch out," said Edith.

No letter came for a long time. And when it did, it was a disappointment. They steamed it open at Edith's house, but found nothing inside for Johanna.

> *Dear Sabitha,*
>
> *Christmas finds me a bit short this year, sorry I don't have more than a two-dollar bill to send you. But I hope you are in good health and have a Merry Christmas and keep up your schoolwork. I have not been feeling so well myself, having got Bronchitis, which I seem to do every winter, but this is the first time it landed me in bed before Christmas. As you see by the address I am in a new place. The apartment was in a very noisy location and too many people dropping in hoping for a party. This is a boardinghouse, which suits me fine as I was never good at the shopping and the cooking.*
>
> *Merry Christmas and love, Dad.*

"Poor Johanna," said Edith. "Her heart will be bwoken."

Sabitha said, "Who cares?"

"Unless we do it," Edith said.

"What?"

"*Answer* her."

They would have to type their letter, because Johanna would notice that it was not in Sabitha's father's handwriting. But the typing was not difficult. There was a typewriter in Edith's house, on a card table in the front room. Her mother had worked in an office before she was married and she sometimes earned a little money still by writing the sort of letters that people wanted to look official. She had taught Edith the basics of typing, in the hope that Edith too might get an office job someday.

"Dear Johanna," said Sabitha, "I am sorry I cannot be in love with you because you have got those ugly spots all over your face."

"I'm going to be serious," said Edith. "So shut up."

She typed, "I was so glad to get the letter—" speaking the words of her composition aloud, pausing while she thought up more, her voice becoming increasingly solemn and tender. Sabitha sprawled on the couch, giggling. At one point she turned on the television, but Edith said, "Pul-eeze. How can I concentrate on my e-motions with all that shit going on?"

Edith and Sabitha used the words "shit" and "bitch" and "Jesus Christ" when they were alone together.

Dear Johanna,

I was so glad to get the letter you put in with Sabitha's and to find out about your life. It must often have been a sad and lonely one though Mrs. Willets sounds like a lucky person for you to find. You have remained industrious and uncomplaining and I must say that I admire you very much. My own life has been a checkered one and I have never exactly settled down. I do not know why I have this inner restlessness and loneliness, it just seems to be my fate. I am always meeting people and talking to people but sometimes I ask myself, Who is my friend? Then comes your letter and you write at the end of it, Your friend. So I think, Does she really mean that? And what a very nice Christmas present it would be for me if Johanna would tell me that she is my friend. Maybe you just thought it was a nice way to end a letter and you don't really know me well enough. Merry Christmas anyway.

Your friend, Ken Boudreau.

The letter went home to Johanna. The one to Sabitha had ended up being typed as well because why would one be typed and not the other? They had been sparing with the steam this time and opened the envelope very carefully so there would be no telltale Scotch tape.

"Why couldn't we type a new envelope? Wouldn't he do that if he typed the letter?" said Sabitha, thinking she was being clever.

"Because a new *envelope* wouldn't have a *postmark* on it. Dumb-dumb."

"What if she answers it?"

"We'll read it."

"Yah, what if she answers it and sends it direct to *him*?"

Edith didn't like to show she had not thought of that.

"She won't. She's sly. Anyway, you write him back right away to give her the idea she can slip it in with yours."

"I hate writing stupid letters."

"Go on. It won't kill you. Don't you want to see what she says?"

Dear Friend,

You ask me do I know you well enough to be your friend and my answer is that I think I do. I have only had one Friend in my life, Mrs. Willets who I loved and she was so good to me but she is dead. She was a lot older than me and the trouble with Older Friends is they die and leave you. She was so old she would call me sometimes by another person's name. I did not mind it though.

I will tell you a strange thing. That picture that you got the photographer at the Fair to take, of you and Sabitha and her friend Edith and me, I had it enlarged and framed and set it in the living room. It is not a very good picture and he certainly charged you enough for what it is, but it is better than nothing. So the day before yesterday I was dusting around it and I imagined I could hear you say Hello to me. Hello, you said, and I looked at your face as well as you can see it in the picture and I thought, Well, I must be losing my mind. Or else it is a sign of a letter coming. I am just fooling, I don't really believe in anything like that. But yesterday there was a letter. So you see it is not asking too much of me to be your friend. I can always find a way to keep busy but a true Friend is something else again.

Your Friend, Johanna Parry.

Of course, that could not be replaced in the envelope. Sabitha's father would spot something fishy in the references to a letter he had never written. Johanna's words had to be torn into tiny pieces and flushed down the toilet at Edith's house.

When the letter came telling about the hotel it was months and months later. It was summer. And it was just by luck that Sabitha had picked that letter up, since she had been away for three weeks, staying at the cottage on Lake Simcoe that belonged to her Aunt Roxanne and her Uncle Clark.

Almost the first thing Sabitha said, coming into Edith's house, was, "Ugga-ugga. This place stinks."

"Ugga-ugga" was an expression she had picked up from her cousins.

Edith sniffed the air. "I don't smell anything."

"It's like your dad's shop, only not so bad. They must bring it home on their clothes and stuff."

Edith attended to the steaming and opening. On her way from the Post Office, Sabitha had bought two chocolate eclairs at the bakeshop. She was lying on the couch eating hers.

"Just one letter. For you," said Edith. "Pore old Johanna. Of course he never actually *got* hers."

"Read it to me," said Sabitha resignedly. "I've got sticky guck all over my hands."

Edith read it with businesslike speed, hardly pausing for the periods.

Well, Sabitha, my fortunes have taken a different turn, as you can see I am not in Brandon anymore but in a place called Gdynia. And not in the employ of my former bosses. I have had an exceptionally hard winter with my chest troubles and they, that is my bosses, thought I should be out on the road even if I was in danger of developing pneumonia so this developed into quite an argument so we all decided to say farewell. But luck is a strange thing and just about that time I came into possession of a Hotel. It is too complicated to explain the ins and outs but if your grandfather wants to know about it just tell him a man who owed me money which he could not pay let me have this hotel instead. So here I am moved from one room in a boardinghouse to a twelve-bedroom building and from not even owning the bed I slept in to owning several. It's a wonderful thing to wake up in the morning and know you are your own boss. I have some fixing up to do, actually plenty, and will get to it as soon as the weather warms up. I will need to hire somebody to help and later on I will hire a good cook to have a restaurant as well as the beverage room. That ought to go like hotcakes as there is none in this town. Hope you are well and doing your schoolwork and developing good habits.

Love, Your Dad.

Sabitha said, "Have you got some coffee?"

"Instant," said Edith. "Why?"

Sabitha said that iced coffee was what everybody had been drinking at the cottage and they were all crazy about it. She was crazy about it too. She got up and messed around in the kitchen, boiling the water and stirring up the coffee with milk and ice cubes. "What we really ought to have is vanilla ice cream," she said. "Oh, my Gad, is it ever wonderful. Don't you want your eclair?"

Oh, my Gad.

"Yes. All of it," said Edith meanly.

All these changes in Sabitha in just three weeks—during the time Edith had been working in the shop and her mother recovering at home from her operation. Sabitha's skin was an appetizing golden-brown color, and her hair was cut shorter and fluffed out around her face. Her cousins had cut it and given her a permanent. She wore a sort of playsuit, with shorts cut like a skirt and buttons down the front and frills over the shoulders in a becoming blue color. She had got plumper, and when she leaned over to pick up her glass of iced coffee, which was on the floor, she displayed a smooth, glowing cleavage.

Breasts. They must have started growing before she went away, but Edith had not noticed. Maybe they were just something you woke up with one morning. Or did not.

However they came, they seemed to indicate a completely unearned and unfair advantage.

Sabitha was full of talk about her cousins and life at the cottage. She would say, "Listen, I've got to tell you about this, it's a scream—" and then ramble on about what Aunt Roxanne said to Uncle Clark when they had the fight, how Mary Jo drove with the top down and without a license in Stan's car (who was Stan?) and took them all to a drive-in—and what was the scream or the point of the story somehow never became clear.

But after a while other things did. The real adventures of the summer. The older girls—that included Sabitha—slept in the upstairs of the boathouse. Sometimes they had tickling fights—they would all gang up on someone and tickle her till she shrieked for mercy and agreed to pull her pajama pants down to show if she had hair. They told stories about girls at board-ing school who did things with hairbrush handles, toothbrush handles. *Ugga-ugga.* Once a couple of cousins put on a show—one girl got on top of the other and pretended to be the boy and they wound their legs around each other and groaned and panted and carried on.

Uncle Clark's sister and her husband came to visit on their honeymoon, and he was seen to put his hand inside her swim-suit.

"They really loved each other, they were at it day and night," said Sabitha. She hugged a cushion to her chest. "Peo-ple can't help it when they're in love like that."

One of the cousins had already done it with a boy. He was one of the summer help in the gardens of the resort down the road. He took her out in a boat and threatened to push her out until she agreed to let him do it. So it wasn't her fault.

"Couldn't she swim?" said Edith.

Sabitha pushed the cushion between her legs. "Oooh," she said. "Feels so nice."

Edith knew all about the pleasurable agonies Sabitha was feel-ing, but she was appalled that anybody would make them pub-lic. She herself was frightened of them. Years ago, before she knew what she was doing, she had gone to sleep with the blan-ket between her legs and her mother had discovered her and told her about a girl she had known who did things like that all the time and had eventually been operated on for the problem.

"They used to throw cold water on her, but it didn't cure her," her mother had said. "So she had to be cut."

Otherwise her organs would get congested and she might die.

"Stop," she said to Sabitha, but Sabitha moaned defiantly and said, "It's nothing. We all did it like this. Haven't you got a cushion?"

Edith got up and went to the kitchen and filled her empty iced-coffee glass with cold water. When she got back Sabitha was lying limp on the couch, laughing, the cushion flung on the floor.

"What did you think I was doing?" she said. "Didn't you know I was kidding?"

"I was thirsty," Edith said.

"You just drank a whole glass of iced coffee."

"I was thirsty for water."

"Can't have any fun with you." Sabitha sat up. "If you're so thirsty why don't you drink it?"

They sat in a moody silence until Sabitha said, in a conciliatory but disappointed tone, "Aren't we going to write Johanna another letter? Let's write her a lovey-dovey letter."

Edith had lost a good deal of her interest in the letters, but she was gratified to see that Sabitha had not. Some sense of having power over Sabitha returned, in spite of Lake Simcoe and the breasts. Sighing, as if reluctantly, she got up and took the cover off the typewriter.

"My darlingest Johanna—" said Sabitha.

"No. That's too sickening."

"She won't think so."

"She will so," said Edith.

She wondered whether she should tell Sabitha about the danger of congested organs. She decided not to. For one thing, that information fell into a category of warnings she had received from her mother and never known whether to wholly trust or distrust. It had not fallen as low, in credibility, as the belief that wearing footrubbers in the house would ruin your eyesight, but there was no telling—someday it might.

And for another thing—Sabitha would just laugh. She laughed at warnings—she would laugh even if you told her that chocolate eclairs would make her fat.

"Your last letter made me so happy—"

"Your last letter filled me with rap-ture—" said Sabitha.

"—made me so happy to think I did have a true friend in the world, which is you—"

"I could not sleep all night because I was longing to crush you in my arms—" Sabitha wrapped her arms around herself and rocked back and forth.

"*No.* Often I have felt so lonely in spite of a gregarious life and not known where to turn—"

"What does that mean—'gregarious'? She won't know what it means."

"*She* will."

That shut Sabitha up and perhaps hurt her feelings. So at the end Edith read out, "'I must say good-bye and the only way I can do it is to imagine you reading this and blushing—' Is that more what you want?"

"Reading it in bed with your nightgown on," said Sabitha, always quickly restored, "and thinking how I would crush you in my arms and I would suck your titties—"

My Dear Johanna,

Your last letter made me so happy to think I have a true friend in the world, which is you. Often I have felt so lonely in spite of a gregarious life and not known where to turn.

Well, I have told Sabitha in my letter about my good fortune and how I am going into the hotel business. I did not tell her actually how sick I was last winter because I did not want to worry her. I do not want to worry you, either, dear Johanna, only to tell you that I thought of you so often and longed to see your dear sweet face. When I was feverish I thought that I really did see it bending over me and I heard your voice telling me I would soon be better and I felt the ministrations of your kind hands. I was in the boardinghouse and when I came to out of my fever there was a lot of teasing going on as to, who is this Johanna? But I was sad as could be to wake and find you were not there. I really wondered if you could have flown through the air and been with me, even though I knew that could not have happened. Believe me, believe me, the most beautiful movie star could not have been as welcome to me as you. I don't know if I should tell you the other things you were saying to me because they were very sweet and intimate but they might embarrass you. I hate to end this letter because it feels now as if I have my arms around you and I am talking to you quietly in the dark privacy of our room, but I must say good-bye and the only way I can do it is to imagine you reading this and blushing. It would be wonderful if you were reading it in bed with your nightgown on and thinking how I would like to crush you in my arms.

L-v-, Ken Boudreau.

Somewhat surprisingly, there was no reply to this letter. When Sabitha had written her half-page, Johanna put it in the envelope and addressed it and that was that.

When Johanna got off the train there was nobody to meet her. She did not let herself worry about that—she had been thinking that her letter might not, after all, have got here before she did. (In fact it had, and was lying in the Post Office, uncollected, because Ken Boudreau, who had not been seriously sick last winter, really did have bronchitis now and for several days had not come in for his mail. On this day it had been joined by another envelope, containing the check from Mr. McCauley. But payment on that had already been stopped.)

What was of more concern to her was that there did not appear to be a town. The station was an enclosed shelter with benches along the walls and a wooden shutter pulled down over the window of the ticket office. There was also a freight shed—she supposed it was a freight shed—but the sliding door to it would not budge. She peered through a crack between the planks until her eyes got used to the dark in there, and saw that it was empty, with a dirt floor. No crates of furniture there. She called out, "Anybody here? Anybody here?" several times, but she did not expect a reply.

She stood on the platform and tried to get her bearings.

About half a mile away there was a slight hill, noticeable at once because it had a crown of trees. And the sandy-looking track that she had taken, when she saw it from the train, for a back lane into a farmer's field—that must be the road. Now she saw the low shapes of buildings here and there in the trees— and a water tower, which looked from this distance like a toy, a tin soldier on long legs.

She picked up her suitcase—this would not be too difficult; she had carried it, after all, from Exhibition Road to the other railway station—and set out.

There was a wind blowing, but this was a hot day—hotter than the weather she had left in Ontario—and the wind seemed hot as well. Over her new dress she was wearing her same old coat, which would have taken up too much room in the suit-case. She looked with longing to the shade of the town ahead, but when she got there she found that the trees were either spruce, which were too tight and narrow to give much shade, or raggedy thin-leaved cottonwoods, which blew about and let the sun through anyway.

There was a discouraging lack of formality, or any sort of organization, to this place. No sidewalks, or paved streets, no imposing buildings except a big church like a brick barn. A painting over its door, showing the Holy Family with clay-colored faces and staring blue eyes. It was named for an unheard-of saint—Saint Voytech.

The houses did not show much forethought in their situation or planning. They were set at different angles to the road, or street, and most of them had mean-looking little windows stuck here and there, with snow porches like boxes round the doors. Nobody was out in the yards, and why should they be? There was nothing to tend, only clumps of brown grass and once a big burst of rhubarb, gone to seed.

The main street, if that's what it was, had a raised wooden walk on one side only, and some unconsolidated buildings, of which a grocery store (containing the Post Office) and a garage seemed to be the only ones functioning. There was one two-story building that she thought might be the hotel, but it was a bank and it was closed.

The first human being she saw—though two dogs had barked at her—was a man in front of the garage, busy loading chains into the back of his truck.

"Hotel?" he said. "You come too far."

He told her that it was down by the station, on the other side of the tracks and along a bit, it was painted blue and you couldn't miss it.

She set the suitcase down, not from discouragement but because she had to have a moment's rest.

He said he would ride her down there if she wanted to wait a minute. And though it was a new kind of thing for her to accept such an offer, she soon found herself riding in the hot, greasy cab of his truck, rocking down the dirt road that she had just walked up, with the chains making a desperate racket in the back.

"So—where'd you bring this heat wave from?" he said.

She said Ontario, in a tone that promised nothing further.

"Ontario," he said regretfully. "Well. There 'tis. Your hotel." He took one hand off the wheel. The truck gave an accompanying lurch as he waved to a two-story flat-roofed building that she hadn't missed but had seen from the train, as they came in. She had taken it then for a large and fairly derelict, perhaps abandoned, family home. Now that she had seen the houses in town, she knew that she should not have dismissed it so readily. It was covered with sheets of tin stamped to look like bricks and painted a light blue. There was the one word HOTEL, in neon tubing, no longer lit, over the doorway.

"I am a dunce," she said, and offered the man a dollar for the ride.

He laughed. "Hang on to your money. You never know when you'll need it."

Quite a decent-looking car, a Plymouth, was parked outside this hotel. It was very dirty, but how could you help that, with these roads?

There were signs on the door advertising a brand of cigarettes, and of beer. She waited till the truck had turned before she knocked—knocked because it didn't look as if the place could in any way be open for business. Then she tried the door to see if it was open, and walked into a little dusty room with a staircase, and then into a large dark room in which there was a billiard table and a bad smell of beer and an unswept floor. Off in a side room she could see the glimmer of a mirror, empty shelves, a counter. These rooms had the blinds pulled tightly down. The only light she saw was coming through two small round windows, which turned out to be set in double swinging doors. She went on through these into a kitchen. It was lighter, because of a row of high—and dirty—windows, uncovered, in the opposite wall. And here were the first signs of life—somebody had been eating at the table and had left a plate smeared with dried ketchup and a cup half full of cold black coffee.

One of the doors off the kitchen led outside—this one was locked—and one to a pantry in which there were several cans of food, one to a broom closet, and one to an enclosed stairway. She climbed the steps, bumping her suitcase along in front of her because the space was narrow. Straight ahead of her on the second floor she saw a toilet with the seat up.

The door of the bedroom at the end of the hall was open, and in there she found Ken Boudreau.

She saw his clothes before she saw him. His jacket hanging up on a corner of the door and his trousers on the doorknob, so that they trailed on the floor. She thought at once that this was no way to treat good clothes, so she went boldly into the room—leaving her suitcase in the hall—with the idea of hanging them up properly.

He was in bed, with only a sheet over him. The blanket and his shirt were lying on the floor. He was breathing restlessly as if about to wake up, so she said, "Good morning. Afternoon."

The bright sunlight was coming in the window, hitting him almost in the face. The window was closed and the air horribly stale—smelling, for one thing, of the full ashtray on the chair he used as a bed table.

He had bad habits—he smoked in bed.

He did not wake up at her voice—or he woke only part way. He began to cough.

She recognized this as a serious cough, a sick man's cough. He struggled to lift himself up, still with his eyes closed, and she went over to the bed and hoisted him. She looked for a handkerchief or a box of tissues, but she saw nothing so she reached for his shirt on the floor, which she could wash later. She wanted to get a good look at what he spat up.

When he had hacked up enough, he muttered and sank down into the bed, gasping, the charming cocky-looking face she remembered crumpled up in disgust. She knew from the feel of him that he had a fever.

The stuff that he had coughed out was greenish-yellow—

no rusty streaks. She carried the shirt to the toilet sink, where rather to her surprise she found a bar of soap, and washed it out and hung it on the door hook, then thoroughly washed her hands. She had to dry them on the skirt of her new brown dress. She had put that on in another little toilet—the *Ladies* on the train—not more than a couple of hours ago. She had been wondering then if she should have got some makeup.

In a hall closet she found a roll of toilet paper and took it into his room for the next time he had to cough. She picked up the blanket and covered him well, pulled the blind down to the sill and raised the stiff window an inch or two, propping it open with the ashtray she had emptied. Then she changed, out in the hall, from the brown dress into old clothes from her suitcase. A lot of use a nice dress or any makeup in the world would be now.

She was not sure how sick he was, but she had nursed Mrs. Willets—also a heavy smoker—through several bouts of bronchitis, and she thought she could manage for a while without having to think about getting a doctor. In the same hall closet was a pile of clean, though worn and faded, towels, and she wet one of these and wiped his arms and legs, to try to get his fever down. He came half awake at this and began to cough again. She held him up and made him spit into the toilet paper, examined it once more and threw it down the toilet and washed her hands. She had a towel now to dry them on. She went downstairs and found a glass in the kitchen, also an empty, large ginger-ale bottle, which she filled with water. This she attempted to make him drink. He took a little, protested, and she let him lie down. In five minutes or so she tried again. She kept doing this until she believed he had swallowed as much as he could hold without throwing up.

Time and again he coughed and she lifted him up, held him with one arm while the other hand pounded on his back to help loosen the load in his chest. He opened his eyes several times and seemed to take in her presence without alarm or surprise—or gratitude, for that matter. She sponged him once more, being careful to cover immediately with the blanket the part that had just been cooled.

She noticed that it had begun to get dark, and she went down into the kitchen, found the light switch. The lights and the old electric stove were working. She opened and heated a can of chicken-with-rice soup, carried it upstairs, and roused him. He swallowed a little from the spoon. She took advantage of his momentary wakefulness to ask if he had a bottle of aspirin. He nodded yes, then became very confused when trying to tell her where. "In the wastebasket," he said.

"No, no," she said. "You don't mean wastebasket."

"In the—in the—"

He tried to shape something with his hands. Tears came into his eyes.

"Never mind," Johanna said. "Never mind."

His fever went down anyway. He slept for an hour or more without coughing. Then he grew hot again. By that time she had found the aspirin—they were in a kitchen drawer with such things as a screwdriver and some lightbulbs and a ball of twine—and she got a couple into him. Soon he had a violent coughing fit, but she didn't think he threw them up. When he lay down she put her ear to his chest and listened to the wheezing. She had already looked for mustard to make a plaster with, but apparently there wasn't any. She went downstairs again and heated some water and brought it in a basin. She tried to make him lean over it, tenting him with towels, so that he could breathe the steam. He would cooperate only for a moment or so, but perhaps it helped—he hacked up quantities of phlegm.

His fever went down again and he slept more calmly. She dragged in an armchair she had found in one of the other rooms and she slept too, in snatches, waking and wondering where she was, then remembering and getting up and touching him—his fever seemed to be staying down—and tucking in the blanket. For her own cover she used the everlasting old tweed coat that she had Mrs. Willets to thank for.

He woke. It was full morning. "What are you doing here?" he said, in a hoarse, weak voice.

"I came yesterday," she said. "I brought your furniture. It isn't here yet, but it's on its way. You were sick when I got here and you were sick most of the night. How do you feel now?"

He said, "Better," and began to cough. She didn't have to lift him, he sat up on his own, but she went to the bed and pounded his back. When he finished, he said, "Thank you."

His skin now felt as cool as her own. And smooth—no rough moles, no fat on him. She could feel his ribs. He was like a delicate, stricken boy. He smelled like corn.

"You swallowed the phlegm," she said. "Don't do that, it's not good for you. Here's the toilet paper, you have to spit it out. You could get trouble with your kidneys, swallowing it."

"I never knew that," he said. "Could you find the coffee?"

The percolator was black on the inside. She washed it as well as she could and put the coffee on. Then she washed and tidied herself, wondering what kind of food she should give him. In the pantry there was a box of biscuit mix. At first she thought she would have to mix it with water, but she found a can of milk powder as well. When the coffee was ready she had a pan of biscuits in the oven.

As soon as he heard her busy in the kitchen, he got up to go to the toilet. He was weaker than he'd thought—he had to lean over and put one hand on the tank. Then he found some underwear on the floor of the hall closet where he kept clean clothes. He had figured out by now who this woman was. She had said she came to bring him his furniture, though he hadn't asked her or anybody to do that—hadn't asked for the furniture at all, just the money. He should know her name, but he couldn't remember it. That was why he opened her purse, which was on the floor of the hall beside her suitcase. There was a name tag sewn to the lining.

Johanna Parry, and the address of his father-in-law, on Exhibition Road.

Some other things. A cloth bag with a few bills in it. Twenty-seven dollars. Another bag with change, which he didn't bother to count. A bright blue bankbook. He opened it up automatically, without expectations of anything unusual.

A couple of weeks ago Johanna had been able to transfer the whole of her inheritance from Mrs. Willets into her bank account, adding it to the amount of money she had saved. She had explained to the bank manager that she did not know when she might need it.

The sum was not dazzling, but it was impressive. It gave her substance. In Ken Boudreau's mind, it added a sleek upholstery to the name Johanna Parry.

"Were you wearing a brown dress?" he said, when she came up with the coffee.

"Yes, I was. When I first got here."

"I thought it was a dream. It was you."

"Like in your other dream," Johanna said, her speckled forehead turning fiery. He didn't know what that was all about and hadn't the energy to inquire. Possibly a dream he'd wakened from when she was here in the night—one he couldn't now remember. He coughed again in a more reasonable way, with her handing him some toilet paper.

"Now," she said, "where are you going to set your coffee?" She pushed up the wooden chair that she had moved to get at him more easily. "There," she said. She lifted him under the arms and wedged the pillow in behind him. A dirty pillow, without a case, but she had covered it last night with a towel.

"Could you see if there's any cigarettes downstairs?"

She shook her head, but said, "I'll look. I've got biscuits in the oven."

Ken Boudreau was in the habit of lending money, as well as borrowing it. Much of the trouble that had come upon him— or that he had got into, to put it another way—had to do with not being able to say no to a friend. Loyalty. He had not been drummed out of the peacetime Air Force, but had resigned out of loyalty to the friend who had been hauled up for offering insults to the C.O. at a mess party. At a mess party, where everything was supposed to be a joke and no offense taken—it was not fair. And he had lost the job with the fertilizer company because he took a company truck across the American border without permission, on a Sunday, to pick up a buddy who had got into a fight and was afraid of being caught and charged.

Part and parcel of the loyalty to friends was the difficulty with bosses. He would confess that he found it hard to knuckle under. "Yes, sir" and "no, sir" were not ready words in his vocabulary. He had not been fired from the insurance company, but he had been passed over so many times that it seemed they were daring him to quit, and eventually he did.

Drink had played a part, you had to admit that. And the idea that life should be a more heroic enterprise than it ever seemed to be nowadays.

He liked to tell people he'd won the hotel in a poker game. He was not really much of a gambler, but women liked the sound of that. He didn't want to admit that he'd taken it sight unseen in payment of a debt. And even after he saw it, he told himself it could be salvaged. The idea of being his own boss did appeal to him. He did not see it as a place where people would stay—except perhaps hunters, in the fall. He saw it as a drinking establishment and a restaurant. If he could get a good cook. But before anything much could happen money would have to be spent. Work had to be done—more than he could possibly do himself though he was not unhandy. If he could live through the winter doing what he could by himself, proving his good intentions, he thought maybe he could get a loan from the bank. But he needed a smaller loan just to get through the winter, and that was where his father-in-law came into the picture. He would rather have tried somebody else, but nobody else could so easily spare it.

He had thought it a good idea to put the request in the form of a proposal to sell the furniture, which he knew the old man would never bestir himself enough to do. He was aware, not very specifically, of loans still outstanding from the past—but he was able to think of those as sums he'd been entitled to, for supporting Marcelle during a period of bad behavior (hers, at a time when his own hadn't started) and for accepting Sabitha as his child when he had his doubts. Also, the McCauleys were the only people he knew who had money that nobody now alive had earned.

I brought your furniture.

He was unable to figure out what that could mean for him, at present. He was too tired. He wanted to sleep more than he wanted to eat when she came with the biscuits (and no cigarettes). To satisfy her he ate half of one. Then he fell dead asleep. He came only half awake when she rolled him on one side, then the other, getting the dirty sheet out from under him, then spreading the clean one and rolling him onto that, all without making him get out of bed or really wake up.

"I found a clean sheet, but it's thin as a rag," she said. "It didn't smell too good, so I hung it on the line awhile."

Later he realized that a sound he'd been hearing for a long time in a dream was really the sound of the washing machine. He wondered how that could be—the hot-water tank was defunct. She must have heated tubs of water on the stove. Later still, he heard the unmistakable sound of his own car starting up and driving away. She would have got the keys from his pants pocket.

She might be driving away in his only worthwhile possession, deserting him, and he could not even phone the police to nab her. The phone was cut off, even if he'd been able to get to it.

That was always a possibility—theft and desertion—yet he turned over on the fresh sheet, which smelled of prairie wind and grass, and went back to sleep, knowing for certain that she had only gone to buy milk and eggs and butter and bread and other supplies—even cigarettes—that were necessary for a decent life, and that she would come back and be busy downstairs and that the sound of her activity would be like a net beneath him, heaven-sent, a bounty not to be questioned.

There was a woman problem in his life right now. Two women, actually, a young one and an older one (that is, one of about his own age) who knew about each other and were ready to tear each other's hair out. All he had got from them recently was howling and complaining, punctuated with their angry assertions that they loved him.

Perhaps a solution had arrived for that, as well.

When she was buying groceries in the store, Johanna heard a train, and driving back to the hotel, she saw a car parked at the railway station. Before she had even stopped Ken Boudreau's car she saw the furniture crates piled up on the platform. She talked to the agent—it was his car there—and he was very surprised and irritated by the arrival of all these big crates. When she had got out of him the name of a man with a truck—a clean truck, she insisted—who lived twenty miles away and sometimes did hauling, she used the station phone to call the man and half bribed, half ordered him to come right away. Then she impressed upon the agent that he must stay with the crates till the truck arrived. By suppertime the truck had come, and the man and his son had unloaded all the furniture and carried it into the main room of the hotel.

The next day she took a good look around. She was making up her mind.

The day after that she judged Ken Boudreau to be able to sit up and listen to her, and she said, "This place is a sinkhole for money. The town is on its last legs. What should be done is to take out everything that can bring in any cash and sell it. I don't mean the furniture that was shipped in, I mean things like the pool table and the kitchen range. Then we ought to sell the building to somebody who'll strip the tin off it for junk. There's always a bit to be made off stuff you'd never think had any value. Then—What was it you had in mind to do before you got hold of the hotel?"

He said that he had some idea of going to British Columbia, to Salmon Arm, where he had a friend who had told him one time he could have a job managing orchards. But he couldn't go because the car needed new tires and work done on it before he could undertake a long trip, and he was spending all he had just to live. Then the hotel had fallen into his lap.

"Like a ton of bricks," she said. "Tires and fixing the car would be a better investment than sinking anything into this place. It would be a good idea to get out there before the snow comes. And ship the furniture by rail again, to make use of it when we get there. We have got all we need to furnish a home."

"It's maybe not all that firm of an offer."

She said, "I know. But it'll be all right."

He understood that she did know, and that it was, it would be, all right. You could say that a case like his was right up her alley.

Not that he wouldn't be grateful. He'd get to a point where gratitude wasn't a burden, where it was natural—especially when it wasn't demanded.

Thoughts of regeneration were starting. *This is the change I need.* He had said that before, but surely there was one time when it would be true. The mild winters, the smell of the evergreen forests and the ripe apples. *All we need to make a home.*

He has his pride, she thought. That would have to be taken account of. It might be better never to mention the letters in which he had laid himself open to her. Before she came away, she had destroyed them. In fact she had destroyed each one as soon as she'd read it over well enough to know it by heart, and that didn't take long. One thing she surely didn't want was for them ever to fall into the hands of young Sabitha and her shifty friend. Especially the part in the last letter, about her nightgown, and being in bed. It wasn't that such things wouldn't go on, but it might be thought vulgar or sappy or asking for ridicule, to put them on paper.

She doubted they'd see much of Sabitha. But she would never thwart him, if that was what he wanted.

This wasn't really a new experience, this brisk sense of expansion and responsibility. She'd felt something the same for Mrs. Willets—another fine-looking, flighty person in need of care and management. Ken Boudreau had turned out to be a bit more that way than she was prepared for, and there were the differences you had to expect with a man, but surely there was nothing in him that she couldn't handle.

After Mrs. Willets her heart had been dry, and she had considered it might always be so. And now such a warm commotion, such busy love.

Mr. McCauley died about two years after Johanna's departure. His funeral was the last one held in the Anglican church. There was a good turnout for it. Sabitha—who came with her mother's cousin, the Toronto woman—was now self-contained and pretty and remarkably, unexpectedly slim. She wore a sophisticated black hat and did not speak to anybody unless they spoke to her first. Even then, she did not seem to remember them.

The death notice in the paper said that Mr. McCauley was survived by his granddaughter Sabitha Boudreau and his son-in-law Ken Boudreau, and Mr. Boudreau's wife Johanna, and their infant son Omar, of Salmon Arm, B.C.

Edith's mother read this out—Edith herself never looked at the local paper. Of course, the marriage was not news to either of them—or to Edith's father, who was around the corner in the front room, watching television. Word had got back. The only news was Omar.

"Her with a *baby*," Edith's mother said.

Edith was doing her Latin translation at the kitchen table. *Tu ne quaesieris, scire nefas, quem mihi, quem tibi—*

In the church she had taken the precaution of not speaking to Sabitha first, before Sabitha could not speak to her.

She was not really afraid, anymore, of being found out—though she still could not understand why they hadn't been. And in a way, it seemed only proper that the antics of her former self should not be connected with her present self—let alone with the real self that she expected would take over once she got out of this town and away from all the people who thought they knew her. It was the whole twist of consequence that dismayed her—it seemed fantastical, but dull. Also insulting, like some sort of joke or inept warning, trying to get its hooks into her. For where, on the list of things she planned to achieve in her life, was there any mention of her being responsible for the existence on earth of a person named Omar?

Ignoring her mother, she wrote, "You must not ask, it is forbidden for us to know—"

She paused, chewing her pencil, then finished off with a chill of satisfaction, "—what fate has in store for me, or for you—"

A woman goes to her doctor to have a prescription renewed. But the doctor is not there. It's her day off. In fact the woman has got the day wrong, she has mixed up Monday with Tuesday.

This is the very thing she wanted to talk to the doctor about, as well as renewing the prescription. She has wondered if her mind is slipping a bit.

"What a laugh," she has expected the doctor to say. "Your mind. You of all people."

(It isn't that the doctor knows her all that well, but they do have friends in common.)

Instead, the doctor's assistant phones a day later to say that the prescription is ready and that an appointment has been made for the woman—her name is Nancy—to be examined by a specialist about this mind problem.

It isn't mind. It's just memory.

Whatever. The specialist deals with elderly patients.

Indeed. Elderly patients who are off their nut.

The girl laughs. Finally, somebody laughs.

She says that the specialist's office is located in a village called Hymen, twenty or so miles away from where Nancy lives.

"Oh dear, a marriage specialist," says Nancy.

The girl doesn't get it, begs her pardon.

"Never mind, I'll be there."

What has happened in the last few years is that specialists are located all over the place. Your CAT scan is in one town and your cancer person in another, pulmonary problems in a third, and so on. This is so you won't have to travel to the city hospital, but it can take about as long, since not all these towns have hospitals and you have to ferret out where the doctor is once you get there.

It is for this reason that Nancy decides to drive to the village of the Elderly Specialist—as she decides to call him—on the evening before the day of her appointment. That should give her lots of time to find out where he is, so there will be no danger of her arriving all flustered or even a little late, creating a bad impression right off the bat.

Her husband could go with her, but she knows that he wants to watch a soccer game on television. He is an economist who watches sports half the night and works on his book the other half, though he tells her to say he is retired.

She says she wants to find the place herself. The girl in the doctor's office has given her directions to the town.

The evening is beautiful. But when she turns off the highway, driving west, she finds that the sun is just low enough to shine into her face. If she sits up quite straight, however, and lifts her chin, she can get her eyes into shadow. Also, she has good sunglasses. She can read the sign, which tells her that she has eight miles to go to the village of Highman. Highman. So that's what it was, no joke. Population 1,553.

Why do they bother to put the 3 on?

Every soul counts.

She has a habit of checking out small places just for fun, to see if she could live there. This one seems to fill the bill. A decent-sized market, where you could get fairly fresh vegetables, though they would probably not be from the fields round about, okay coffee. Then a Laundromat, and a pharmacy, which could fill your prescriptions even if they didn't stock the better class of magazines.

There are signs of course that the place has seen better days. A clock that no longer tells the time presides over a window which promises Fine Jewellery but now appears to be full of any old china, crocks and pails and wreaths twisted out of wires.

She gets to look at some of this trash because she has chosen to park in front of the shop where it is displayed. She thinks that she may as well search out this doctor's office on foot. And almost too soon to give her satisfaction she does see a dark brick one-story building in the utilitarian style of the last century and she is ready to bet that is it. Doctors in small towns used to have their working quarters as part of their houses, but then they had to have space where cars could park, and they put up something like this. Reddish-brown bricks, and sure enough the sign, Medical/Dental. A parking lot behind the building.

In her pocket she has the doctor's name and she gets out the scrap of paper to check it. The names on the frosted glass door are Dr. H. W. Forsyth, Dentist, and Dr. Donald McMillen, Physician.

These names are not on Nancy's piece of paper. And no wonder, because nothing is written there but a number. It is the shoe size of her husband's sister, who is dead. The number is O 7½. It takes her a while to figure that out, the O standing for Olivia but scribbled in a hasty way. She can only recall faintly something about buying slippers when Olivia was in the hospital.

That's no use to her anyway.

One solution may be that the doctor she will see has newly moved into this building and the name on the door has not been changed yet. She should ask somebody. First she should ring the bell on the off chance that somebody is in there, working late. She does this, and it is a good thing in a way that nobody comes, because the doctor's name that she is after has for a moment slipped below the surface of her mind.

Another idea. Isn't it quite possible that this person—the crazy-doctor, as she has chosen to call him in her head—isn't it quite possible that he (or she—like most people of her age she does not automatically allow for that possibility) that he or she does operate out of a house? It would make sense and be cheaper. You don't need a lot of apparatus for the crazy doctoring.

So she continues her walk away from the main street. The doctor's name that she is after has come back to her, as such things are apt to do when there is no longer a crisis. The houses she walks by were mostly built in the nineteenth century. Some of wood, some of brick. The brick ones often two full stories high, the wooden ones somewhat more modest, a story and a half with slanting ceilings in the upstairs rooms. Some front doors open just a few feet from the sidewalk. Others onto wide verandas, occasionally glassed in. A century ago, on an evening like this one, people would have been sitting on their verandas or perhaps on the front steps. Housewives who had finished washing the dishes and sweeping up the kitchen for the last time that day, men who had coiled up the hose after giving the grass a soaking. No garden furniture such as now sat here empty, showing off. Just the wooden steps or dragged-out kitchen chairs. Conversation about the weather or a runaway horse or some person who has taken to bed and was not expected to recover. Speculation about herself, once she was out of earshot.

But wouldn't she have put their minds at ease by this time, stopping and asking them, Please, can you tell me, where is the doctor's house?

New item of conversation. What does she want the doctor for?

(This once she has put herself out of earshot.)

Now every single person is inside with their fans on or their air-conditioning. Numbers on the houses appear, just as in a city. No sign of a doctor.

Where the sidewalk ends there is a large brick building with gables and a clock tower. Perhaps a school, before the children were bused to some larger and drearier center of learning. The hands stopped at twelve, for noon or midnight, which certainly is not the right time. Profusion of summer flowers that seem professionally arranged—some spilling out of a wheel-barrow and more out of a milk pail on its side. A sign she cannot read because the sun is shining straight onto it. She climbs up on the lawn to see it at another angle.

Funeral Home. Now she sees the built-on garage that probably holds the hearse.

Never mind. She had better get on with things.

She turns onto a side street where there are very well kept places indeed, proving that even a town this size can have its suburb. The houses all slightly different yet somehow looking all the same. Gently colored stone or pale brick, peaked or rounded windows, a rejection of the utilitarian look, the ranch style of past decades.

Here there are people. They haven't all managed to shut themselves up with the air-conditioning. A boy is riding a bicycle, taking diagonal routes across the pavement. Something about his riding is odd, and she cannot figure it out at first.

He is riding backward. That's what it is. A jacket flung in such a way that you could not see—or she cannot see—what is wrong.

A woman who might be too old to be his mother—but who is very trim and lively looking all the same—is standing out in the street watching him. She is holding on to a skipping rope and talking to a man who could not be her husband—both of them are being too cordial.

The street is a curved dead end. No going farther.

Interrupting the adults, Nancy excuses herself. She says that she is looking for a doctor.

"No, no," she says. "Don't be alarmed. Just his address. I thought you might know."

Then comes the problem of realizing that she is still not sure of the name. They are too polite to show any surprise at this but they cannot help her.

The boy on one of his perverse sallies comes swinging around, barely missing all three.

Laughter. No reprimand. A perfect young savage and they seem to positively admire him. They all remark on the beauty of the evening, and Nancy turns to go back the way that she has come.

Except that she does not go all the way, not as far as the funeral home. There is a side street she ignored before, perhaps because it was unpaved and she had not thought of a doctor living in such circumstances.

There is no sidewalk, and the houses are surrounded with trash. A couple of men are busy under the hood of a truck, and she has an idea it would not do to interrupt them. Besides, she has glimpsed something interesting ahead.

There is a hedge that comes right out to the street. It is high enough that she does not expect to be able to see over it, but thinks she might be able to peek through.

That is not necessary. When she gets past the hedge she finds that the lot—about the size of four town lots—is quite open to the road she is walking on. It appears to be some sort of park, with flagstone paths diagonally crossing the mown and flourishing grass. In between the paths, and bursting from the grass, there are flowers. She knows some of them—the dark gold and light yellow daisies for instance, pink and rosy and red-hearted white phlox—but she is no great gardener herself and here there are clumped or trailing displays of all colors that she could not name. Some of them climb trellises, some spread free. Everything artful but nothing stiff, not even the fountain that shoots up seven feet or so before falling down into its rock-lined pool. She has walked in off the street to get a little of its cool spray, and there she finds a wrought-iron bench, where she can sit down.

A man has come along one of the paths, carrying a pair of shears. Gardeners are evidently expected to work late here. Though to tell the truth, he does not look like a hired workman. He is tall and very thin and dressed in a black shirt and pants that tightly fit his body.

It has not occurred to her that this could be anything but a town park.

"This is   really beautiful," she calls to him in her most assured and approving voice. "You keep it up so well."

"Thank you," he says. "You're welcome to rest there."

Informing her by some dryness of voice that this is not a park but private property, and that he himself is not a village employee but the owner.

"I should have asked your permission."

"That's okay."

Preoccupied, bending and snipping at a plant that is encroaching on the path.

"It's yours, is it? All of it?"

After a moment's busyness, "All of it."

"I should have known. It's too imaginative to be public. Too unusual."

No answer. She is going to ask him whether he likes to sit here himself, in the evenings. But she better not bother. He doesn't seem an easy person to be around. One of those who pride themselves, probably, on that very fact. After a moment she will thank him and get up.

But instead, after a moment he comes and sits down beside her. He speaks just as if a question has been put to him.

"Actually, I only feel comfortable when I'm doing something that needs attending to," he says. "If I sit down I have to keep my eyes off everything, or I'll just see some more work."

She should have known right away that he was a man who doesn't like banter. But still she is curious.

What was here before?

Before he made the garden?

"A knitting factory. All these little places had something like that, you could get away with the starvation wages then. But in time that went under and there was a contractor who thought he was going to turn it into a nursing home. There was some trouble then, the town wouldn't give him a license, they had some idea there'd be a lot of old people around and make it depressing. So he set fire to it or he knocked it down, I don't know."

He's not from around here. Even she knows that if he was he'd never talk so openly.

"I'm not from around here," he says. "I had a friend who was, though, and when he died I came up just to get rid of the place and go."

"Then I got hold of this land cheap because the contractor had left it just a hole in the ground and it was an eyesore."

"I'm sorry if I seem inquisitive."

"That's all right. If I don't feel like explaining something I don't do it."

"I haven't been here before," she says. "Of course I haven't, or I'd have seen this spot. I was walking around looking for something. I thought I could find it better if I parked my car and walked. I was looking for a doctor's office, actually."

She explains about not being sick, just having an appointment tomorrow, and not wanting to be running around in the morning looking for the place. Then she tells him about parking her car and being surprised that the name of the doctor she wanted was not listed anywhere.

"I couldn't look in the phone book either because you know how the phone books and the phone booths have all disappeared now. Or else you find their insides ripped out. I'm beginning to sound quite silly."

She tells him the name of the doctor, but he says it doesn't ring a bell.

"But I don't go to doctors."

"You're probably just as smart not to."

"Oh, I wouldn't say that."

"At any rate, I'd better get back to my car."

Standing up when she does, he says he will walk with her.

"So I won't get lost?"

"Not altogether. I always try to stretch my legs this time of the evening. Garden work can leave you cramped."

"I'm sure there's some sensible explanation about this doctor. Do you ever think that there used to be more sensible explanations about things than there are now?"

He does not answer. Thinking perhaps of the friend who died. The garden perhaps a memorial to the friend who died.

Instead of being embarrassed now when she has spoken and

he has not answered, she feels a freshness, a peace in the conversation.

They walk along without meeting a soul.

Soon they reach the main street, with the medical building just a block away. The sight of it makes her feel somewhat less easy, and she does not know why, but after a moment she does. She has an absurd but alarming notion that the sight of the medical building has provoked. What if the right name, the name she said she could not find, has been waiting there all along. She moves more quickly, she finds that she is shaky, and then, having quite good eyesight she reads the two useless names just as before.

She pretends to have been hurrying to look at the assortment in the window, the china-headed dolls and ancient skates and chamber pots and quilts already in tatters.

"Sad," she says.

He is not paying attention. He says that he has just thought of something.

"This doctor," he says.

"Yes?"

"I wonder if he might be connected with the home?"

They are walking again, passing a couple of young men sitting on the sidewalk, one with his legs stretched out so they have to move around him. The man with her takes no notice of them, but his voice has dropped.

"Home?" she says.

"You wouldn't have noticed if you came in from the highway. But if you keep going out of town towards the lake you pass it. Not more than half a mile out. You go past the gravel pile on the south side of the road and it's just a little farther on, on the other side. I don't know if they have a live-in doctor there or not, but it stands to reason they might have."

"They might have," she says. "It stands to reason."

Then she hopes he doesn't think she is copying him on purpose, making a silly joke. It is true that she wants to go on talking to him longer, silly jokes or whatever.

But now comes another of her problems—she has to think about the whereabouts of her keys, as she often does before getting into the car. She is regularly worried about whether she's locked the keys inside or dropped them somewhere. She can feel the approach of familiar, tiresome panic. But then she finds them, in her pocket.

"It's worth a try," he says, and she agrees.

"There's plenty of room to turn off the road and take a look. If there's a doctor out there regularly, there's no need for him to have his name up in town. Or her name, as the case might be."

As if he too is not entirely anxious for them to part.

"I have you to thank."

"Just a hunch."

He holds the door while she gets in, and closes it, waits there until she is turned to go in the right direction, then waves good-bye.

When she is on her way out of the town she catches sight of him again in the rearview mirror. He is bending over, speaking to the couple of boys or young men who were sitting on the pavement with their backs against the wall of the store. He had ignored them in such a way that she is surprised to see him talking to them now.

Maybe a remark to be made, some joke about her vagueness or silliness. Or just her age. A mark against her, with the nicest man.

She had thought that she would come back through the village to thank him again and tell him if it was the right doctor. She could just slow down and laugh and call out the window.

But now she thinks that she will just take the lakeshore route and stay out of his way.

Forget him. She sees the gravel pile coming up, she has to pay attention to where she is going.

Just as he has said. A sign. A notice of the Lakeview Rest Home. And there really is, from here, a view of the lake, a thread of pale blue along the horizon.

A spacious parking lot. One long wing with what looks like separate compartments, or good-sized rooms at least, with their own little gardens or places to sit. A latticed fence quite high in front of every one of them for privacy, or safety. Though nobody is sitting out there now that she can see.

Of course not. Bedtime comes early in these establishments.

She likes how the lattice provides a touch of fantasy. Public buildings have been changing in the past few years, just as private houses have. The relentless, charmless look—the only one permitted in her youth—has disappeared. Here she parks in front of a bright dome that has a look of welcome, of cheerful excess. Some people would find it fakey, she supposes, but isn't it the very thing you would want? All that glass must cheer the spirits of the old people, or even, perhaps, of some people not so old but just off kilter.

She looks for a button to push, a bell to ring, as she walks up to the door. But that is not necessary—the door opens on its own. And once she gets inside there is an even greater expression of space, of loftiness, a blue tinge to the glass. The floor is all silvery tiles, the sort that children love to slide on, and for a moment she thinks of the patients sliding and slipping for pleasure and the idea makes her light-hearted. Of course it cannot be as slippery as it looks, you wouldn't want people breaking their necks.

"I didn't dare try it myself," she says in a charming voice to somebody in her head, perhaps her husband. "It wouldn't have

done, would it? I could have found myself in front of the doctor, the very one who was getting ready to test my mental sta-
bility. And then what would he have to say?"

At the moment there is no doctor to be seen.

Well, there wouldn't be, would there? Doctors don't sit
behind desks here waiting for patients to show up.

And she isn't even here for a consultation. She will have to
explain again that she is making sure of the time and place of
an appointment for tomorrow. All this has made her feel rather
tired.

There is a rounded desk, waist high, whose panels of dark
wood look like mahogany, though they probably are not.
Nobody behind it at the moment. It is after hours of course.
She looks for a bell but does not see one. Then she looks to see
if there is a list of doctors' names or the name of the doctor in
charge. She doesn't see that either. You would think there
would be a way of getting hold of somebody, no matter what
the hour. Somebody on call in a place like this.

No important clutter behind the desk either. No computer
or telephone or papers or colored buttons to press. Of course
she has not been able to get right behind the desk, there may
well be some lock, or some compartments she can't see. Buttons a receptionist could reach and she can't.

She gives up on the desk for the moment, and takes a closer
look at the space she has found herself in. It's a hexagon, with
doors at intervals. Four doors—one is the large door that lets in
the light and any visitors, another is an official and private-
looking door behind the desk, not that easy of access, and the
other two doors, exactly alike and facing each other, would
obviously take you into the long wings, to the corridors and
rooms where the inmates are housed. Each of these has an
upper window, and the window glass looks clear enough for
anybody to manage to see through.

She goes up to one of these possibly accessible doors and knocks, then tries the knob and cannot budge it. Locked. She cannot see through the window properly, either. Close up the glass is all wavy and distorted.

In the door directly opposite there is the same problem with the glass and the same problem with the knob.

The click of her shoes on the floor, the trick of the glass, the uselessness of the polished knobs have made her feel more discouraged than she would care to admit.

She does not give up, however. She tries the doors again in the same order, and this time she shakes both knobs as well as she can and also calls out, "Hello?" in a voice that sounds at first trivial and silly, then aggrieved, but not more hopeful.

She squeezes herself in behind the desk and bangs that door, with practically no hope. It doesn't even have a knob, just a keyhole.

There is nothing to do but get out of this place and go home.

All very cheerful and elegant, she thinks, but there is no pretense here of serving the public. Of course they shove the residents or patients or whatever they call them into bed early, it is the same old story everywhere, however glamorous the surroundings.

Still thinking about this, she gives the entry door a push. It is too heavy. She pushes again.

Again. It does not budge.

She can see the pots of flowers outside in the open air. A car going by on the road. The mild evening light.

She has to stop and think.

There are no artificial lights on in here. The place will get dark. Already in spite of the lingering light outside, it seems to be getting dark. No one will come, they have all completed their duties, or at least the duties that brought them through this part of the building. Wherever they have settled down now is where they will stay.

She opens her mouth to yell but it seems that no yell is forthcoming. She is shaking all over and no matter how she tries she cannot get her breath down into her lungs. It is as if she has a blotter in her throat. Suffocation. She knows that she has to behave differently, and more than that, she has to believe differently. Calm. Calm. Breathe. Breathe.

She doesn't know if the panic has taken a long time or a short time. Her heart is pounding but she is nearly safe.

There is a woman here whose name is Sandy. It says so on the brooch she wears, and Nancy knows her anyway.

"What are we going to do with you?" says Sandy. "All we want is to get you into your nightie. And you go and carry on like a chicken that's scared of being et for dinner.

"You must have had a dream," she says. "What did you dream about now?"

"Nothing," says Nancy. "It was back when my husband was alive and when I was still driving the car."

"You have a nice car?"

"Volvo."

"See? You're sharp as a tack."

Your Majesties, Your Royal Highnesses, Esteemed Laureates,
Ladies and Gentlemen,

It may seem like a paradox, but it is actually quite logical:
What we call world literature is generally rooted in the local
and individual. In her writing, Alice Munro portrays with
almost anthropological precision a recognizable, tranquil every-
day world with predictable external accoutrements; her equiva-
lent of William Faulkner's Yoknapatawpha County is located in
southwestern Ontario. This flat Canadian agricultural land-
scape, with its broad rivers and seemingly bland small towns, is
where most of her short stories unfold. But the serenity and
simplicity are deceptive in every way.

The tranquillity of the outer world is always apparent in
Alice Munro's works, which then open the portals to an inner
world where the opposite is true. Munro writes about what are
usually called ordinary people, but her intelligence, compas-
sion and astonishing power of perception enable her to give
their lives a remarkable dignity—indeed redemption—since
she shows how much of the extraordinary can fit into that
jam-packed emptiness called The Ordinary. The trivial and

trite are intertwined with the amazing and unfathomable—but never at the cost of contradiction. If you have never before fantasized about the strangers you see on a bus, you begin doing so after having read Alice Munro.

Her short stories rely very little on external drama. They are an emotional chamber play, a world of silences and lies, waiting and longing. The biggest events occur inside of her characters. The greatest pain remains unexpressed. Like few others, she is interested in the silent and the silenced, the passive, those who choose not to choose, who live on the sidelines, the quitters and losers. Barriers of gender and class are never far away in her works.

In the mental topography that is Munro's own, what might have happened is often just as important as what actually happened. Of key importance are all the things her characters could not or did not wish to understand there and then, but that only long afterward stand revealed, at best in the form of an epiphany. She shows that our innermost self is essentially inaccessible to other people, often eluding even ourselves— until it is too late.

In an uncompromising way, Alice Munro demonstrates that love rarely saves us or leads to reliable happiness, and that few things can be as devastating to us as our own dreams. Sexuality is constantly present and its power is gripping, but often blind and even devastating. Even though genuine happiness may occur, sometimes accidentally, people rarely go unpunished for believing in romantic love. This might seem unbearably dark, or even painful, if her piercing lucidity were not mixed with something that—for want of a better word—I must call tenderness. If you read a lot of Alice Munro's works carefully, sooner or later, in one of her short stories, you will come face to face with yourself; this is an encounter that always leaves you shaken and often changed, but never crushed.

The seemingly prosaic surface level in Alice Munro's short stories is interwoven in an interesting way with her writing style and distinctive storytelling technique. The minimalist style we encounter is clean, transparent, subtle, and stunningly precise. It is a challenge to find an unessential word or a superfluous phrase. Reading one of her texts is like watching a cat walk across a laid dinner table. A brief short story can often cover decades, summarizing a life, as she moves deftly between different periods. No wonder Alice Munro is often able to say more in thirty pages than an ordinary novelist is capable of in three hundred. She is a virtuoso of the elliptical and—as the Academy said in its brief prize citation—the master of the contemporary short story.

Over the years, numerous prominent scientists have received their well-deserved reward in this auditorium for having solved some of the great enigmas of the universe or of our material existence. But you, Alice Munro, like few others, have come close to solving the greatest mystery of them all: the human heart and its caprices.

The Swedish Academy congratulates you. I now ask Jenny Munro to rise and, in her mother's place, receive the 2013 Nobel Prize in Literature from the hand of His Majesty the King.

Given at the 2013 Nobel Prize Award Ceremony in Stockholm on December 10, 2013, by Professor Peter Englund, Permanent Secretary of the Swedish Academy

ALSO BY ALICE MUNRO

THE BEGGAR MAID

In this exhilarating series of interweaving stories, Alice Munro re-creates the evolving bond—one that is both constricting and empowering—between two women in the course of almost forty years. One is Flo, practical, suspicious of other people's airs, at times dismayingly vulgar. The other is Rose, Flo's stepdaughter, a clumsy, shy girl who somehow—in spite of Flo's ridicule and ghastly warnings—leaves the small town she grew up in to achieve her own equivocal success in the larger world.

Fiction/Short Stories

OPEN SECRETS

In *Open Secrets*, Munro uncovers the devastating power of old love suddenly recollected. She tells of vanished young schoolgirls, indentured frontier brides, an eccentric recluse who finds love at a dinner party, and a Canadian woman fleeing a husband and a lover. These stories resonate with sorrow, humor, and wisdom, confirming Munro as one of the most gifted writers of our time.

Fiction/Short Stories

THE LOVE OF A GOOD WOMAN

Mining the silences and dark discretions of provincial life, these tales lay bare the seamless connections and shared guilt that bind even the loneliest individuals. Munro evokes the vagaries of love, the tension and deceit that lie in wait under the polite surfaces of society, and the strange, often comical desires of the human heart.

Fiction/Short Stories

HATESHIP, FRIENDSHIP, COURTSHIP, LOVESHIP, MARRIAGE

In the nine stories that make up this celebrated collection, Alice Munro achieves new heights, creating narratives that loop and swerve like memory, and conjuring up characters as thorny and contradictory as people we know ourselves. This is Munro at her best—tirelessly observant, serenely free of illusion, and deeply humane.

Fiction/Short Stories

THE VIEW FROM CASTLE ROCK

A young boy, taken to Edinburgh's Castle Rock to look across the sea to America, catches a glimpse of his father's dream. Scottish immigrants experience love and loss on a journey that leads them to rural Ontario. Wives, mothers, fathers, and children move through uncertainty, ambivalence, and contemplation in these stories of hope, adversity, and wonder. *The View from Castle Rock* reveals what is most essential in Munro's art: her compassionate understanding of ordinary lives.

Fiction/Short Stories

THE PROGRESS OF LOVE

A divorced woman returns to her childhood home and confronts the memory of her parents' confounding yet deep bond. The accidental near-drowning of a child exposes the fragility of the trust between children and parents. A man brings his lover on a visit to his ex-wife, only to feel unexpectedly closer to his estranged partner. Drawing us into the most intimate corners of ordinary lives, Munro reveals much about ourselves, our choices, and our experiences of love.

Fiction/Short Stories

ALSO AVAILABLE

Away from Her
Carried Away
Dance of the Happy Shades
Dear Life
Friend of My Youth
Lives of Girls and Women
The Moons of Jupiter
Runaway
Selected Stories
Something I've Been Meaning to Tell You

VINTAGE INTERNATIONAL
Available wherever books are sold.
www.vintagebooks.com